Paris Pan takes the DARE

Paris Pan takes the DARE

Cynthea Liu

G. P. Putnam's Sons · Penguin Young Readers Group

For Clara. See the possibilities.

G. P. PUTNAM'S SONS
A division of Penguin Young Readers Group.
Published by The Penguin Group. Penguin Group (USA) Inc., 375 Hudson Street, New York, NY 10014, U.S.A. Penguin Group (Canada), 90 Eglinton Avenue East, Suite 700, Toronto, Ontario M4P 2Y3, Canada (a division of Pearson Penguin Canada Inc.). Penguin Books Ltd, 80 Strand, London WC2R 0RL, England. Penguin Ireland, 25 St. Stephen's Green, Dublin 2, Ireland (a division of Penguin Books Ltd.). Penguin Group (Australia), 250 Camberwell Road, Camberwell, Victoria 3124, Australia (a division of Pearson Australia Group Pty Ltd). Penguin Books India Pvt Ltd, 11 Community Centre, Panchsheel Park, New Delhi—110 017, India. Penguin Group (NZ), 67 Apollo Drive, Rosedale, North Shore 0632, New Zealand (a division of Pearson New Zealand Ltd). Penguin Books (South Africa) (Pty) Ltd, 24 Sturdee Avenue, Rosebank, Johannesburg 2196, South Africa. Penguin Books Ltd, Registered Offices: 80 Strand, London WC2R 0RL, England.

Published simultaneously in Canada. Printed in the United States of America.
Design by Richard Amari.
Text set in Egyptienne Roman.

Library of Congress Cataloging-in-Publication Data
Liu, Cynthea. Paris Pan takes the dare / Cynthea Liu. p. cm. Summary: Friendless because of her family's frequent moves, twelve-year-old Chinese American Paris Pan wants very much to fit in with the seemingly friendly girls in her new school, even if it means taking a dare to spend the night in a spooky woods, reputedly haunted by the ghost of a girl who died there years ago. [1. Friendship—Fiction. 2. Moving, Household—Fiction. 3. Interpersonal relations—Fiction. 4. Schools—Fiction. 5. Conduct of life—Fiction. 6. Chinese Americans—Fiction.] I. Title.
PZ7.L739325Par 2009 [Fic]—dc22 2008036511

ISBN 978-0-399-25043-9
1 3 5 7 9 10 8 6 4 2

ACKNOWLEDGMENTS

I'd like to thank my agent, Jen, and my writing buddies, Tammi Sauer and Beverly Patt—all of whom believed in Paris Pan, even when I was having one of those "special" moments.

Karen and Nicole, my editors, who saw all the good in Paris Pan and worked hard to make her even better. No, let's edit that—perfect.

My fans Cali, Ashlee, and Tyler Kinder, who want to prove to their friends that they know a REAL author. Here's the proof. (Now, where's my cut?)

My husband, Mark, and the rest of the Schoenhals family—Betty, Floyd, Amy, and Joel. Thanks for supporting me through the craziness!

Finally, I want to thank my mom, Helen, dad, Raymond, brother, William, and sister, Veronique—the real Pans in my life, only slightly quirkier and perhaps a little bit funnier. Without the Lius, there would be no Pans.

Paris Pan
takes the
DARE

chapter 1

Where should I start? The first time I felt my life hanging in the balance? Or the moment I believed the deceased had a way of talking to me? Or maybe I ought to begin with the second I walked into that school.

Looking back, I should have been suspicious from day one, but now I know that when you want something badly enough, you'll do anything to get it.

You'll lie to your friends.

Steal from your family.

Eat a *whole* box of orange Creamsicles.

You might even go as far as taking the Dare.

But now I'm getting ahead of myself, so let's start from the beginning—my first day at Sugar Lake Elementary.

The principal and I walked down the hall to my seventh-grade classroom. "Paris Pan," Mr. Carlisle said, "it's not every day we get a new student. I'm sure Mrs. Wembly's class will be more than eager to meet you."

We stopped in front of a door, and he bent down to look me in the eye. His big forehead shined under the fluorescent lights. "You play basketball, Miss Pan?"

I wrinkled my face and shook my head. What a weird question.

"Well, little girl . . ." Mr. Carlisle leaned in. "You'll learn.

Basketball is *very* important here. We'll make something out of you one way or another." He straightened.

I faked a smile.

There was no way I was playing basketball.

Mr. Carlisle swung open the door. Then he gave me a shove, and the door smacked shut behind me.

The teacher noticed me right away, and man, did I notice her. She was wearing a giant sweater in crosswalk yellow and pink pants. "You must be our new student," she said brightly as she led me to the front of the room. "Class, meet Paris Pan."

I counted the kids staring back at me.

Seven boys. Three girls.

This was the entire seventh grade?

"Who wants to get Paris a desk?"

Two boys jumped up and raced to the back of the room. They grabbed empty desks and dragged them up the aisles. Mr. Carlisle wasn't kidding—these people were desperate for someone new.

I took off my backpack and studied the two boys pushing furniture toward me. One of them was cute, though he could definitely use less hair gel. The other boy was as skinny as a green bean and just as plain to look at. I picked the desk touched by the cuter boy and slid into the seat. A squabble quickly erupted over the other desk.

"Jay! Tom!" Mrs. Wembly tapped at the board. "Sit down."

Somehow, Cute Boy won and plunked down beside me. I guessed his name must be Jay since Mrs. Wembly had said his name and glared at him first. His lanky friend Tom scraped another desk across the floor and pulled up to my right. My neighbors studied me like I was a museum piece. I felt their gaze move from the top of my ponytailed head, down to my straight-cut bangs, to my flat nose and pointed chin. I fidgeted in my seat.

"You Japanese?" Jay whispered.

I inwardly groaned. Just because I have "almond-shaped" eyes and black hair does not mean I say *sayonara* and eat sushi. I tried to pretend I was invisible, but this was some challenge in my sister's hand-me-down jacket. Verona thought everything should be hot pink.

Mrs. Wembly turned toward us, math problems on the board behind her. "Tom, what's one hundred percent of one hundred?"

One hundred, duh! Obviously, a trick question.

"Tom?"

I looked at Tom. He was searching the depths of his brain.

A hundred, just say it. Say it.

"Zuh-zuh-zuh-zero?"

Holy moly! But what made me really wince was the way he said his answer. His speech impediment was fifty times worse than how my parents talked, and they spoke *Chinese.* I rested my forehead in my hands, wondering how I was going to get through the rest of the day. I should have done more to stop us from moving this time—like lying in front of the U-Haul instead of the usual hunger strike.

It was only a few days ago, at the end of January, when

my parents slapped the Sold sticker on the sign in our front yard. Daddy builds each house we live in, and before the paint has a chance to dry, he sells it and moves us to the next one. And it doesn't matter what time of year it is either. Right before school ends. After it starts. Mid-semester. Daddy always says, "When house close, we go," and go we do.

I've led a nomadic lifestyle since I was eight. That was when Daddy quit a corporate job as a construction manager and started building homes on his own. This means I change houses about every seven or eight months, which has resulted in three things. One, in the middle of the night, I've almost gone to the bathroom in a closet twice. Two, my school transcript is longer than any Harry Potter book. And three, my lifelong friend roster has only one name on it—my dog's.

Nevertheless, Daddy and Mom assured us Sugar Lake was not just another move. They insisted that this place would be nothing like we'd seen before, and they proved it when we took the tour.

I sat wedged between my siblings in the backseat of our car. Verona jabbed me in the ribs. "Scoot over!"

I jabbed her back. "Can I help it if your rear takes up a zip code?"

"Paris!" My brother, Athens, pushed my arm. "Your elbow is over the line."

We passed a sign that said *Sugar Lake, Oklahoma. Where Life Is Sweet!* I studied the stretch of land before me. Empty was more like it. The area was nothing like

Tulsa, the last city I called home. Or Topeka, the city before that. Or even Branson, the town before that. Where were the expressways? The traffic lights? *The curbs?* We passed one dirt road after another. RR 2, RR 9, RR 15— even the streets weren't named after anything. In twenty minutes, we saw only three places: Foster's Woods, the actual Sugar Lake, and the town center—a line of old buildings and a beat-up gas station.

"No mall?" Verona whined.

"No movie theater?" Athens said.

"No nothing," I concluded.

We kept going and came upon two more buildings. Daddy stopped the car.

"Children," he said, "left is elementary. Right is high school for Athens."

Athens gaped at a building that looked more like a rusted warehouse than an institute for higher education. Above the doors, a banner featured a picture of a bumblebee announcing, *The Big Sting: Boys Basketball 7 and 0.*

The Sugar Lake mascot was a dribbling insect. *Great.*

"Um, Daddy?" Verona said. "Where's the middle school?"

"Left!" he replied.

I looked hard for a building that wasn't labeled *Sugar Lake Elementary*. "Where?"

Mom, sitting in the front seat, read from a piece of paper. "There! Sugar Lake Elementary. Grade K through eight."

Verona and I studied a shoe box of a school across the street. Then we stared at each other. "No way!"

So here I was, sitting in a classroom at a school of only ninety-seven people, learning what a hundred percent of anything was.

I checked the room for clues I was in the wrong place—possibly the third grade—when a tiny wad of paper suddenly landed on my desk.

Someone was trying to communicate.

I put my hand over the wad, slid it to my lap, and opened it.

Wanna have lunch? TYPTTFY = tap your pencil two times for yes. And I don't take no for an anser. Mayo

Mayo? And what happened to the *w* in *answer*? I glanced over my shoulder. A girl with dark red hair and freckles sprinkled across her nose grinned back at me. I bit my lip and did the math: lunch with one person was better than lunch with no one.

I tapped my pencil twice.

When the bell rang for lunch, I stood up as Cute Boy and his friend, the rocket scientist, closed in on me. The rest of the kids got their coats and headed outside.

Tom put out his hand. "Huh-huh-hi."

Before I could respond, Mayo stepped in front of me. "Leave her alone, Tom. She's having lunch with *me.*" She gripped my wrist and pulled me toward the door.

When we got outside, she let go of me at the top of some steps and tugged on her jacket. She stood tall, nose up and chest out. The country air and country food had treated her well in all departments.

I rubbed my wrist. "Thanks." I think.

"Tom plus Jay equals Stu-pid, Paris." She flipped her hair over her shoulder. "Don't let them dumbify you."

The boys walked by. Jay puckered his lips at us, which changed my mind about how cute he was.

Mayo shook her fist at him. "Keep your lips out of our way, or I'll let you have it!"

"I'd like to see you try." Jay smooched the air again and winked. "C'mon, Tom." They headed down the stairs. Tom glanced back at me.

"Loose Lips and his dimwit sidekick are trouble, Paris." Mayo sat on the bottom of the steps and pulled me down with her. "You got that?"

I nodded and surveyed the school yard: children scrambling all over rusty playground equipment—a tetanus epidemic just waiting to happen.

"I know it's not much," Mayo said, gesturing at the staircase. "But at least these steps are ours."

"Hey, Paris." A girl I recognized from class sat beside me. "I'm Dana." She set down her lunch bag. With big blue eyes and dark, long lashes, Dana looked so innocent, like Bambi.

"So has Mayo figured out if you're a freak yet?"

"Dana!" Mayo said.

"I was just kidding." Dana studied me. "So where's your lunch?"

I shrugged. "Um, in the cafeteria?"

"You're funny, Paris," Mayo said. "We don't have a cafeteria. Here." She handed me half a ham sandwich, then dumped some Cheetos on her lunch bag. "The first thing you have to learn here is that we girls stick together. In a school this size, friends are few and far between. Isn't that right, Dana?"

"Yup."

And so the lessons on "How to Survive Sugar Lake Elementary" began.

First, the school yard. Mayo mapped out the grounds by dragging a stick through the mud, pointing here and there as she laid out the territory. "The benches by the fence are where the seventh-grade boys prowl. But don't bother with them; they have the IQs of fish. The picnic tables are where the eighth graders hang, and if they bother to speak to you, don't trust them. It's a setup . . ."

I spotted my sister at the tables, with new friends circling her like paparazzi. While I have always been the wallflower at every new school, Verona is usually the It girl. She has that indefinable quality that draws people to her like monkeys to a banana. Where she got It from in our family, I have no idea.

I glanced away and listened to Mayo. I needed to focus on building up my own posse.

". . . and the playground equipment," Mayo continued, "is reserved strictly for *children.* Don't be caught dead near any of them. Kids in grades below us are, well . . ."

"Below us," Dana finished.

I nodded. It made sense.

Mayo stabbed the stick toward one end of the yard. "And *that* over there should be avoided. *At all costs.*"

My gaze followed the stick to where another girl from our class was sitting in a tire swing that hung from an oak tree. "Why?" I said.

"Paris, are you blind?" Mayo jerked her head toward the tree. "Can't you spot the school reject when you see her?"

"Oh." I studied the girl. I hadn't paid much attention to her in class. I had only noticed she was sitting closest to the teacher's desk. Her hair was done up in Pippi Long-stocking braids, and she was reading a book—no one within twenty feet of her. Her face was so pale, she looked like she was made of chalk.

"That's Robin," Mayo said.

"It's so embarrassing that she's in our grade," Dana added.

Mayo shook her head. "What a *freak.*"

The way she said *freak* made me flinch. "What's wrong with her?" I hoped we didn't have too much in common.

"All she does is rock in that swing with some book."

I swallowed. I loved reading.

"But that's not her only problem." Dana sucked the last ounce from her juice box.

"No, it isn't." Mayo pointed a finger to her ear and did the cuckoo sign. "That girl is mental."

"Mental?" I studied Robin harder. Aside from the pasty complexion, she looked normal to me. "What do you mean?"

"First of all," Mayo said, "the braids and the jumper she's wearing under that dumpy coat should be a major tip-off. But in case you need more proof, Robin hardly ever talks. I can probably count up the number of words she's said this year on my fingers."

I raised a brow. That was a little odd.

"Yeah, and get this, Paris," Dana said. "Mrs. Wembly pretends like that's okay—"

"Like she's normal when she's SO not," Mayo said.

I was getting the picture. "You mean she's like . . . uh . . . verbally challenged or something?"

"Yeah, that's putting it nicely," Mayo said. "I don't care what you call it—*challenged, freak,* same thing. Mental."

Phew!—my similarities with Robin ended at the books. I had no problems talking. My fatal flaw was embarrassing myself by talking.

Mayo dropped a rock on the dirt. "This represents Robin's tree." She drew a wide circle around it. "Do not enter the Freak Zone. Understand?"

Understand? Oh yes. At every school, there's at least one freak. Often I feared that freak would become me, being the new kid and all. But fortunately, I'd been on quite a lucky streak. Someone else had always been more worthy. At the last school, it was a sixth grader who had a terrible overbite and had to wear headgear. The school before, it was a fifth grader who must have weighed five hundred pounds. So at Sugar Lake, it made sense that Robin—the wordless wonder—was the shoo-in. I smoothed my hair and tried to sound cool. "I totally understand."

"Great." Mayo tossed the stick and dusted off her hands. "Dana, I think Paris will do. What do you think?"

"Three's a magic number," Dana said.

"All right, then." Mayo smiled. "I hereby declare ourselves a trio until further notice."

Whoa. Wait a second. I was in?

Mayo leaned forward and shifted her knees toward me. "Now there's something we'd like to ask."

Mayo and Dana looked at me expectantly.

"What?"

"I'm having a birthday party," Mayo said. "Wanna come?"

"Birthday party?" She was inviting *me*?

"I'll be thirteen on Friday, the fifth," Mayo announced.

"But it's no party when you have only two people," Dana said. "Can you make it?"

I did everything in my power to remain calm—Mayo and Dana were presenting an opportunity I rarely encountered.

Perhaps there were benefits to living in a speck of a town.

Perhaps the mere fact that I represented twenty-five percent of the female population in the seventh grade was a good thing.

Perhaps I, Paris Pan, after four years of moving, was finally friendship material.

I turned to Mayo and smiled. "What should I bring?"

"Well, a present, I hope, and a change of clothes. It's a sleepover."

"Bring a flashlight, too," Dana added.

"Flashlight?" I said.

"Dana, not a word," Mayo warned.

Dana shot Mayo a look. "I wasn't going to say anything." She scooted in close. "Are you afraid of ghosts, Paris?"

"Dana!" Mayo flung a Cheeto at her. "Friday." She elbowed me. "When we can tell you in private."

"Sounds great to me," I said, like I had no idea about huddling under blankets and telling ghost stories.

Mayo talked about her birthday party theme while I finished my sandwich. I glanced at Robin swinging back and forth with her book. Seeing that girl made me glad I'd made it into Mayo's circle of friends.

chapter 2

After an afternoon of lessons I'd already learned last year, I decided this would be my first and final day sitting in the front row. Mayo and Dana had opened the communication lines, and everyone had been hurling notes at me. One from Jay that said, *Meet me by the water fountain after school.* One from Tom that said, *Sorry about Jay.* And too many to count from Mayo and Dana. *Don't listen to those boys. TTIYGTM = tap twice if you get the message.*

Finally, the school bell rang, and I headed for the exit with my new friends. Younger kids pushed past us through the doors toward a bus parked outside.

"You coming with us?" Mayo said as she and Dana followed the pack.

"No," I said. "I've got my own ride, thanks."

Mayo frowned. "Huh?" She glanced at the bus. "No, I meant b-ball practice."

"Excuse me?"

"Basketball." Dana pointed at the high school across the road. "The gym?"

"Nah," I said. "I'm going home."

Dana stared at me, wide-eyed. "Really? You're not going to practice?"

"Um, why would I?"

Mayo laughed. "New girl," she said, nodding to Dana. "She'll learn soon enough." She smiled at me. "We'll see you tomorrow."

As I watched them walk away, wondering what exactly I was going to learn, giggles erupted behind me. I turned to see my sister stepping out of the building with her flock. I whirled around and did what any self-respecting sister would do—pretend we weren't related.

A car horn honked. Athens was at the curb, revving the engine of the family Buick. He adjusted his sunglasses and scowled like we were making him late for an important date. (And this boy has never had a date.) I headed to the car. From the look of my brother's clenched jaw, I could tell he was still fuming about last night. Mom said he had to let Verona and me ride with him if he wanted to use the car for school. He made a thing of it, but I knew the real reason why he didn't want to cart us around: the Pan sisters cramped his style.

I opened the door. "Hey."

"Get in," Athens grunted.

"What did you think I was going to do next?"

"Shut up, Paris. I said, get in."

I grumbled as I climbed into the backseat and shut the door. I looked out the window and watched the Verona fan club hanging on my sister's every word while Her Highness bid her adieus.

My brother honked again.

Verona turned, giving him the evil eye she has spent

years perfecting. She turned back to her friends, a last kiss was delivered on the final cheek, and she got into the car.

"What's your hurry, Athens?" She slammed her door and smiled at the club through the window. "Don't you know how important it is to make a good first impression?"

"Do I care?" Athens said, spinning the tires against the mud. The car jolted forward.

I eyed the club waving their good-byes. "Verona, what did you tell them this time? That some movie star is your real sister? Or you're the princess of Taiwan on a visit to their rich and beautiful city?"

Verona turned from the front seat, and I was horrified by the blue eye shadow that caked her nonexistent lids. "You're just jealous because I'm infinitely more popular than you are," she said.

"No, Verona, I'm just glad I don't need enough makeup for a circus to make friends like you do."

Athens groaned. "Would you dork wads just shut up?"

"You shut up!" my sister and I said in unison. The only bond Verona and I share is our common dislike for Athens. Athens loves to pretend we don't exist. The Verona part, I understand. But me? My brother and I used to be like *this,* and by that I mean I could always count on him to help me lock Verona in a closet for hours. Of course, everything changed when Athens went to high school. He outgrew me like I outgrew crayons. I sighed. I guess it didn't matter anyway. Next year he'd be off to college, and I'd become a distant memory.

None of us said another word the rest of the way. That was probably because Athens had cranked up the radio so loud, I could feel my teeth vibrate. I focused on the wintry scene outside. We were surrounded by the woods—the trees were bare, and dried leaves littered the ground. Sugar Lake slowly came into view, looking abandoned by the cold. I wondered what summer was like here. Did kids swim in the lake? Did families have cookouts beside it and shoot fireworks in July? Then I realized I might be gone again before I could find out, so I stopped wondering.

The trees broke on my right, making way for a one-lane road. A mailbox labeled *The Coxes* stood at the entrance. Farther down was a two-story frame house with a small parking lot in the front. A sign read *Johnny's Bait and Tackle*. (*You bait 'em, we tackle the rest!*) After that, there were no other houses, just the hill I lived on.

We went up the slope, and before it dead-ended into the woods, Athens pulled into our gravel driveway. Nestled in the trees, our work-in-progress ranch-style home greeted us. I say work-in-progress because Daddy hasn't totally finished it yet, but so far this lovely abode sports four bedrooms, three-and-a-half baths, a two-car garage, an open floor plan, stainless steel appliances, and granite countertops. *It's city living in the country at its best!* I could already see the real estate ad.

In fact, this would be the ad. I'm the one who helps Daddy write them.

Athens parked the Buick out front—forget the garage. My father's construction tools took up half of it, and the space left was reserved for our parents to use. But Daddy wouldn't be using it for another week. He was working on the next project in Choctaw. I could only imagine how thrilling that place would be.

We went into the house and took off our shoes. One rule about our house: take off your shoes or face Mom's wrath should a fleck of dirt touch the carpet. I placed mine neatly by the door, while Verona and Athens headed for their rooms. Mom was still at work. She's a computer programmer in Tulsa, commuting forty-five minutes every day, to make the real bucks in the family. I once believed we ought to be rich from Daddy's houses, but it doesn't work that way. In fact, the more homes my father builds, the poorer we get.

Daddy had explained it like this. "We build equity in house. Then borrow equity. Build bigger house. When last house is sold, then we have money."

I didn't understand my father's explanation. Building equity sounded a lot like gambling to me, and we weren't winning.

I stepped into the living room and found Go, our terrier, whining at the patio door.

"Do you need to go, Go?" I love saying that. *Go* means "dog" in Chinese, but the name fits in English, too. Go always has to go. I put my shoes back on, hooked her up to her retractable leash, and let her into the yard.

Actually, I shouldn't call our yard a yard. Aside from six square feet of patio, it's the woods, twenty acres of it, and I knew exactly how my parents got the land so cheap.

One, it's in the middle of nowhere. Two, there's still a hundred-year-old, run-down shed tucked in those trees, which means the house that was here was no gem. And three, since when have my parents bought anything that *wasn't* cheap?

Go padded through the woods and picked her perfect spot. After she was done, I wiped the mud from her paws and let her inside.

With Go following me, I walked down a bare-walled hall. We're not allowed to put up anything. Mom thinks marks on the wall tell the world the house was "used" before it went up for sale. Never mind the fact that we'd still be living here when potential buyers came through.

I closed the door to my bedroom and sighed at my un-packed boxes and the other things I still hadn't put away. I sighed again when I heard Princess Taipei blabbing on the phone with one of her new best friends. Daddy didn't install extra insulation like I'd asked, so now I got to lis-ten to Verona debate which was better: Maybelline or CoverGirl?

I slid my violin case under my bed. The one good thing about this town is that there isn't a violin teacher within thirty square miles. Mom said Verona and I still had to practice, but *whatever*! I waved the instrument good-bye.

Next, I hoisted two boxes marked *Paris's STUFF* onto my bed. Actually, they should have said *Verona's OLD CLOTHES* because that's what was in them. Sweaters from two seasons ago ... last summer's shorts. I put everything from the first box away, then worked my way down the second. At the very bottom, I found something I never knew what to do with—a flimsy photo album titled *My Memories.*

It'd been a while since I looked at this. It wasn't a typical photo album. It was more like a workbook with questions about my family, my friends, and me. There were blanks to fill in and places to tape pictures. I opened the album's cover and saw my name, scrawled in my happy eight-year-old handwriting.

Back then, Daddy worked long hours for his corporate job, but he came home every day. As for Mom, she's been working like crazy since I can remember. But still, they managed to make time for us. In my album, under the "Things I Do with My Family" section, I'd written . . . *rent a movie, order in pizza, and bowl at Lucky Strike!* I'd taped a photo of the Pan Five, standing together in front of the lanes—Daddy with a hot dog in one hand, Athens giving Verona bunny ears, and Mom with an arm around me.

I flipped the page, and the next picture was of me playing Skee-Ball. Daddy had taken it on my eighth birthday. I'd invited my best friend Shana over, but she'd gotten sick and couldn't come, and Mom, who had planned to take the night off, was called in to work. That evening as I sulked in my room, my father came in and said, "Baby, how about you and me, huh?" He took me out for a night of fun. I'd never been to a real arcade before, and I knew Mom would think it was too expensive. But Daddy said, "I worry about your mother. You worry about the game, okay?" I won a million tickets that night and turned them in for five grape-scented erasers. It was one of my best birthdays ever.

It wasn't long after that when Daddy started his own business, and soon there was less time and less money for everything. We stopped doing stuff as a family. I had to say good-bye to my town, my school, and—I turned to the "Friends" section of the album—my buddies. Aside from Shana, I hardly remembered their names.

I flipped through the album again. There were so many pages to fill. Maybe the next picture under the "Friends" section would be Mayo, Dana, and me. *Maybe.* I smiled as I placed the album on my bookshelf, and when I turned to put away the box, I heard a tapping sound coming from my window.

Go growled and jumped on top of a small box. She rested her paws on the windowsill.

There it was again. *Tapping.*

Go growled louder.

I went to the window and peeked through the blinds. My eyes adjusted to the darkness.

It was Tom.

Stalking me?

I yanked up the blinds and stared hard at him, remembering what Mayo had said. *Don't let them dumbify you.* I nudged Go out of the way and opened the window. The cold air rushed in.

"What are you doing here?" I said.

Tom shrugged. "I just wanted to say h-h-hi is all." He pointed a thumb over his shoulder. "I live j-j-just down the hill. Past Johnny's? I've been w-w-watching your house come up."

So he was stalking me, and he was taking forever to say it.

"And?"

Tom looked uncomfortable. He tried to say something else, but it didn't seem like it was going to come out anytime soon.

Go barked.

Seconds ticked by.

Okay. "Well, thanks for the welcome," I said, "but I've got things to do—"

Bang! I heard my door slam against the wall.

"Paris!" Verona said. "Who are you talking to?"

I turned. My sister was standing in the doorway, her pink phone in her hand.

"Um, no one."

"Well, you and your imaginary friend need to shut it." She shook her phone at me. "How am I supposed to have a decent conversation with you yakking next door?"

"Verona, you don't know what a decent conversation is." I piped up so her peon on the phone could hear. "Don't you have a mustache to bleach or something?"

Verona's tiny eyes bugged out of her head. She slammed my door shut.

Which was exactly how I liked it.

I turned to my window, only Tom wasn't there anymore. Yup, Verona's face was enough to scare off anyone. I closed the window and went back to my boxes, then noticed the room felt eerily quiet.

Something wasn't right.

I looked around me. *"Go?"* I peeked under my bed. She wasn't there. I opened the door to the hallway. No Go. I fixed my gaze on the open window. *She didn't.*

She did. I could make out the outline of her behind disappearing into the trees.

I jerked the window open. "Go!" I stuck my hand out. What happened to the screen? I looked up. It was sitting in the top half of the frame.

Stupid!

I put on the closest shoes I could find—Verona's old sandals—grabbed a jacket, then jumped outside. Within two seconds, my shoes got stuck in the mud. I had to leave them behind.

Lovely—my socks were thick with cold mud.

"Go!" I listened for her collar. Her tags jingled nearby.

"Go, come back here!" The winter sun had faded. I could see only the outlines of the trees and the run-down shed in the middle of it all.

Adrenaline kicked in.

"Go!" I yelled. "Dinner's ready!"

That should get her attention.

Her collar jingled again, but it sounded farther away, and it was coming from the direction of the shed.

I clenched my hands into fists. *Perfect.* Just where I wanted to go. I stepped into a network of branches and made my way over. "Go, dinnertime! *Chi fan le!*" I hoped the bilingual emphasis might bring her out. Go did not appear.

Now I was close enough to the shed that I could see its broken, rotted boards. The dusty windows watched me like eyes in a jack-o'-lantern. My heart pounded.

Go jingled again. This time the sound was closer but in a different direction.

"Go, please!" I moved past the shed. My feet were practically numb. I stopped and listened.

Nothing but the sound of my own breathing.

Go barked behind me.

I whirled around, ready to catch her, but my dog wasn't there.

Someone grabbed my wrist, and I screamed.

"P-P-Paris, it's me!"

I stopped screaming and looked right into Tom's gray eyes; Go yipped under his arm.

"What the heck do you think you're doing, you—you stuttering psycho?!" I shouted.

Tom dropped my wrist and looked away.

I couldn't believe I'd said that. I knew I should take back every word, but I didn't know how to take back something that mean. I only stood there in my muddy socks and stupid jacket like a total idiot.

Go whimpered under Tom's arm. She agreed.

I was an imbecile.

Finally, Tom held out his hand. "Let me h-h-help you."

I took it even though his kind gesture drove a stake through my black heart.

Tom steadied me as we picked through the woods. I tried to find the words to apologize. *I don't think you're psycho.* No . . . *You don't stutter that badly.* No . . .

When we reached my window, I took Go from Tom, dropped her inside, and commanded her to stay. I avoided looking at Tom, afraid he'd see right into my loser core. "Um, I . . ."

I still didn't know what to say, so I went on about Mayo's party on Friday instead.

Tom glanced over his shoulder. "Listen, I b-b-better go. Before it g-g-gets too dark."

I stared at the trees. To me, it was already too dark. "Okay," I said.

Yeah, that was all I could come up with.

"Hey, Paris?"

"What?"

"I know y-y-you didn't mean wh-wh-what you said."

I looked at Tom. The light from my room shined on his face. His eyes weren't gray; they were a wolf-like blue.

"And I didn't mean to s-s-scare you," he went on. "I had to sneak up on y-y-your dog to catch her. That's all." He turned to go.

"Tom, wait."

He stopped and faced me.

"I . . ."

I must have had my mouth open a full minute, maybe longer.

"I'll see you tomorrow."

Tom's shoulders sagged. "Yeah, t-t-tomorrow."

He pushed a branch out of the way and disappeared into the trees.

I sighed, then peeled off my nasty socks and slipped into my room. I looked down at Go, who was surrounded by muddy paw prints in the carpet, something Mom would kill me for, but I didn't care.

I stared right into my dog's black marble eyes. "I'm sorry."

Go whined.

Yeah, that didn't sound like enough.

chapter 3

That night, I decided my mouth was incapable of speaking kind and heartfelt words, so I gave my hand a shot at writing an apology. After twelve different versions of "I'm sorry for calling you a stuttering psycho," I settled on this one.

> *Dear Tom,*
> *My stupid mouth is far worse than*
> *the way you talk. I'm sorry.*
> > *Thanks for catching Go.*
> > *Paris*

At school the next day, I promoted myself to the back row, and during Mrs. Wembly's history lesson about the first moon landing, I tossed my note toward Tom. Of course, being as coordinated as I am, my precious words sailed across his desk and into Jay's lap.

Jay flashed me a pretty-boy smile with a matching wink while I wilted in my chair. He read the note, and his smile vanished. He shot Tom a quizzical look. All I could see was the back of Tom's head, turning to stare at Jay. Jay stifled a laugh.

"Jay!" Mrs. Wembly paused at the blackboard. "What's so funny?"

The entire seventh grade looked at him. Jay pointed to a poster of an astronaut on the wall. "I was just thinking how funny it is that Neil Armstrong had big feet. That was one giant step, all right."

A couple of kids chuckled, and Mrs. Wembly frowned before she launched into a lecture on Armstrong's finer points.

Jay tossed Tom the note, and I pretended to be engrossed in whatever Mrs. Wembly was saying. A wad of paper landed on my desk. It was from Mayo.

R U kissing on J?

I looked at Mayo, sitting on my right, and mouthed a big *no*. She didn't seem satisfied with my answer.

Dana, on my left, sent her own note, though she had no idea what we were talking about.

Don't forget your flashlite! Only two more days. Yay! ICW = I can't wait. BTW, Mayo wants a BB = Black Beauty book for her b-day. The fancy kind with the leather cover. You want to split the cost? Ten bucks each.

Mayo wanted a book? Well, who was I to hinder her education? Though the money would be an issue. I'd have to work on Mom, but hopefully she'd understand. If I begged. A lot.

I waited until Mrs. Wembly's back was turned and nodded a yes to Dana. But when I looked in her direction, I caught Tom staring at me. He was sitting in front of Dana, one row up and to the left, so I knew it wasn't some accidental glance.

My face heated up and I looked away.

● ● ●

That evening, Verona and I stood at the stove, making our usual brain-nourishing dinner—macaroni and cheese. Of course, my sister had a pot to herself as did I. No need to risk contamination. A female voice from the TV echoed through the kitchen. Mom was at the dining table, working on her books again. On top of her computer job in Tulsa, she manages the family finances, including Daddy's project stuff. This is her routine: come home from work, flip on the TV, and hack away at invoices, receipts, bank statements . . . She never watches what's on the set. In the past, I've flipped the channel to *Sesame Street,* hoping Mom might absorb some basic English, but she still has no idea what the word *the* is for.

My sister reached around me for the milk carton and turned it upside down over her pot. Nothing came out. I smiled.

"You hogged the milk!" Verona said.

I held back a laugh as I stirred my very creamy pasta.

"Paris!" My sister tried to grab my pot.

"Stop it!" I said. "I'll share."

I scooped out a portion into a bowl and let Verona have the rest. But the battle wasn't over. I let Go lick my spoon, and just as Verona started to scoop out *my* macaroni, I stuck the slobbery utensil into the pot.

My sister got so mad, she melted at least two of the five layers of makeup on her face. "You are so disgusting!" She slammed down the pot and stormed out with an empty stomach. Which was exactly how I liked it.

Now that I had Mom alone, I decided it would be an excellent time to discuss an important financial matter.

I set down my bowl and stood in front of the dining table. "Mom?"

"Yes?" She didn't look up from her ledger.

"Can you spot me ten?"

"Do you mean I give you ten dollars?" She put a finger on a page and punched numbers into the calculator.

"Yes, Mom, ten dollars."

"Ten dollars?"

I rolled my eyes. *Where's a translator when you need one?* "Yes, ten dollars!"

"Baby, don't yell. I right here. What you need ten dollars for?"

"A birthday present," I said. "A friend invited me to a slumber party Friday."

Mom kept her gaze on her work. "Party? Who this friend?"

"Mayo."

"What name is that?"

"Mo-om," I moaned. "I hate to tell you this, but our names aren't exactly normal either."

"You right." She flipped the page in her ledger. "Your daddy's idea. He wants you children go places."

"So?" I said. "Can I have ten dollars? *Please?*" I rested my hands on the edge of her books. "I haven't been invited to a real birthday party in like *forever.*"

Mom glanced up with a tired look on her face. "Baby, you a good girl, and I like to help, but this time, you make something. More special that way. We don't have ten dollars here, ten dollars there." She directed her scowl toward her papers, and that was the end of the conversation.

With Go close behind, I grabbed my bowl of mac and cheese and headed for my room. I tried not to let my mother's answer get to me, but that was impossible. Ten dollars was the insurance I needed so everything would go right on Friday.

I wasn't hungry anymore, so I gave my dinner to Go. Then I opened my book boxes. Maybe *Black Beauty* had somehow made it into my collection. I whipped out the *Encyclopedia of Infectious Diseases, How to Win Friends and Influence People, Health and Wellness* . . .

My personal library was built on garage sales and library discards—*surprise, surprise.* I mostly owned stuff I needed to supplement my education, such as books that provided advice on matters I did not want from any Pan. I shelved *Look Natural, Look Beautiful* next to *Rules of the Road: A Driver's Manual.* When I got to the last one,

Psychology Today: Staying Sane in the 21st Century, I sighed. Nothing with talking horses.

While I was at it, I unloaded my Muppet plush toys and placed them at the end of each shelf. Though I know I'm a little old to like this kind of stuff, the cast of *Sesame Street* holds a special place in my heart. I've watched a million episodes since I was a baby because some people had no qualms about leaving my upbringing to puppets.

"So, Bert? What do I do?"

Bert just gave me a blank look.

Fine. Mom was right. I was going to have to make something for Mayo—it was more special that way. Just how special was up to me.

Since the birthday girl wouldn't be working on her reading, I figured the next-best thing would be her writing. I grabbed some things from around my room and set out to construct a journal out of cardboard, notebook paper, yarn, and Magic Markers. I was doomed.

I pulled my notebook from my backpack and started to rip pages from it for Mayo's journal.

A square of paper slipped from the notebook and fell to the floor.

I picked it up.

Dear Paris,
No more notes in class—your pitch needs work.
There is something I want to tell you. It's sort of serious. Best if said in person. I'll stop by tomorrow night.
Tom

What serious secret could Tom have?

Maybe body snatchers were taking over the town and I was next.

Or . . . *Sugar Lake's inhabitants were members of a goat-sacrificing cult . . .*

Or no, better yet . . . I looked around my room. *My brand-new house is haunted.* Ha.

I opened my desk drawer and hid the note behind my stapler. It was kind of special—my first scrap of paper from a boy, and his spelling was decent for someone with a serious math disability.

Now I had a journal to make. I dug around in my desk for my Snuffleupagus pen. *Work your magic, baby.*

For the next two hours, Snuffy and I toiled over the cover of Mayo's journal. I tried to sketch a horse. Who said being a lefty meant I could draw? I stared at the giant, dog-like creature with a diamond on its forehead and cringed.

After I was done, I headed for the shower to get ready for bed. While I scrubbed, I fantasized about the best outcome for Mayo's party on Friday. I'd just given her my work of art. Her hands fly to her mouth. Tears of joy flow from her eyes. Then good food and good times.

Someone pounded on the door. "Paris!"

I ignored my sister and cranked up the hot water. *Hmm, should I bring a camera to the party?*

More pounding.

I wonder if Mom would let me use the Polaroid. That

way I can stick the photo right in my album. I shook my head. I could already hear Mom saying, "Each picture, thirty-seven cents!"

I waited until the water started to turn cold and got out.

When I unlocked the bathroom, Verona burst in. "It's about time!"

I went back to my room, and a moment later, my sister shouted—"You used all the hot water!"

I smiled and turned off the light. Go hopped into bed, taking her spot at my feet. I heard my door squeak open.

"Mom, I didn't run the water on purpose," I mumbled. "I swear."

No one replied.

I opened my eyes. "Mom?" My vision focused in the dark. The bedroom door wasn't open.

Bang! Something slammed shut. *Outside.*

Go lifted her head from her paws.

I went to my window and peeked through the blinds. The moon cast its light through the bare trees and onto the shed.

Eeeeeeeer. The shed door swung open.

I took in a breath.

Bang! The sound came from behind me.

I screamed. Go barked.

"Paris!"

I turned around as the lights flipped on.

Athens was at my door. "Man, you are such a doofus. It's just me."

I glared at my brother. "What do you want?"

Athens walked into my room and snooped around my boxes.

"Hey!"

"There it is." He carried a box out of my room. "You had some of my stuff, stupid."

Mom showed up at the doorway. "Baby, why you shout?"

I pursed my lips. "Athens scared me. That's all."

My mother frowned. "Go to bed, Baby. No more noise, okay?" She closed my door.

I went back to the window, with Go at my heels. I peeked through the blinds again. A breeze shook the trees, and the shed door swung closed.

I let the blinds snap into place. "Go," I said.

She cocked her head.

"There's nothing out there but Mother Nature."

I turned off the light and climbed back into bed. Go returned to her spot. I had more important things to think about than *wind*. I imagined myself giggling over a birthday cake with my friends. Maybe I would "borrow" Mom's camera. I glanced at my album on my bookshelf, closed my eyes, and fantasized about pages and pages filled with pictures.

chapter 4

Just before lunch, when Mrs. Wembly's back was turned, I tossed a note to Dana, telling her I didn't have the money for Mayo's gift. Dana looked bummed, then replied Mayo would have to settle for a change purse instead. I had begun to write my response when Mayo dropped a note on my desk.

What are you ladies talking about?

My answer:

Your birthday present S-U-R-P-R-I-S-E.

Mayo was happy with this reply. I almost felt sorry for her. She had no idea a deformed Black Beauty journal and a plastic coin purse were in her future.

The lunch bell rang. I let Mayo and Dana know I had to go to the ladies' room and that they could head outside without me. After the classroom had cleared, I hurried to Tom's desk, opened his history book to the chapter we were on, and slipped in my message.

Why don't we meet somewhere private so no one sees us and thinks we're together? No offense, but who wants to deal with that rumor?

P.S. My backpack isn't safe for notes. My sister thinks it's her office supply store, so unless you want the eighth graders making fun of us, don't leave anything there.

P.P.S. Also, don't write our names in notes in case someone gets ahold of one. Let's find a more secure place to exchange our future communiqué. Somewhere no one would think of looking. Any ideas?

Satisfied, I grabbed my lunch from my backpack and quickly joined Mayo and Dana on our steps.

"So, Paris," Mayo said, "are you ready for some b-ball?"

"B-ball?" I pulled out my sandwich. What was up with this town and basketball?

"We're playing Liberty Hill next week." Dana sighed. "We are gonna get whupped."

"We are not gonna get whupped," Mayo said. "Not with our new star player."

"Yeah?" I took a bite from my PB&J. "Who's this star?"

Mayo wagged a finger at me. "You."

"Me?" The peanut butter in my mouth became sludge. "You're kidding."

"Oh no, missy," Mayo said. "You are on the team."

"Since when?"

"Since you set foot in this school." Mayo unwrapped a Fruit Roll-Up. "Principal Carlisle won't let you get out of this one. Dana, didn't you see Coach Dobson add her to the roster yesterday?"

Dana nodded. "It won't be long now."

Coach Dobson? Was that the woman I saw this morning in the hall—sizing me up?

"Carlisle and the coach are grooming us to be stars by the time we hit high school," Mayo explained. "And besides, if every girl in fifth through eighth grades didn't play, we wouldn't have a team."

"Basketball is practically a requirement," Dana said.

I frowned at my sandwich. "It sounds more like a conspiracy. I can't believe I don't have a choice."

"Actually, you do have a choice, Paris," Mayo said. "You can go to practice tomorrow or spend extra time before school in the gym, stretching for the coach."

I groaned and caught sight of Verona and her gal pals at their picnic bench, trading lipsticks. *Wait a second.* I gestured at the eighth-grade tables. "They're on the team, too?"

"Yup." Mayo wound one end of the Roll-Up around her finger and took a bite. "I said everyone."

The frown on my face gave way to a smile. I could live with the news. But Verona? She'd die.

"Hang on, Mayo." Dana pointed her chin at Robin. "*She's* not a Bumblebee."

"I stand corrected," Mayo said. "Everyone, except Freak. She must like to stretch for the coach."

Dana and Mayo laughed, and I laughed right along with them. Though I didn't know what was so funny.

After lunch, when class started, I watched Tom intently as we opened our history textbooks. He glanced back at me and I knew he'd gotten my note. Now I just had to wait for a reply. When we moved on to English, Tom volunteered to hand back a writing assignment from yesterday. He placed mine on my desk, and I smiled at the big A+ from Mrs. Wembly. *Was there any doubt?*

I then noticed a slip of paper behind my work.

Check the hollow in Robin's tree after school.

Tom was a genius.

When class let out, I said good-bye to Mayo and Dana and waited until everyone headed to the bus. Then I snuck to the back of the school yard and looked over both shoulders before I reached inside the forbidden oak.

I found a square of paper.

Meet me at the lake—4:30 p.m. today. The fishing shack at the end of the dock.

I knew exactly what Tom was talking about. From our house, I could see the lake and the dock if I stared through the trees hard enough. All I had to do was go down the hill on my bike and I'd be there in no time.

Athens took Verona and me home, and at four fifteen, I went to the garage and pushed out my bike. I'd be back no later than six, way before Mom got home. The sun had already begun to set as I rode down the slope. I reached the bottom, and lights glowed from the windows of Johnny's Bait and Tackle. I took a turnoff for the lake, following a path lined with more bare trees. When I reached the dock, I rolled my bike across the planks. A rusted metal building with a tin roof stood at the end. My body tensed. The shack didn't look much better than the shed in my yard.

Tom must have heard me because he stepped out of the building.

"I said to find a place that was private," I told him. "Not freaky."

"I d-d-didn't have much of a choice, Paris." Tom moved my bike inside. "It was h-h-here or the cemetery."

Oh.

I followed him in and stamped my feet to shake off the cold. I frowned at the smell. *Fish.*

While Tom set my bike next to his against the wall, I leaned over a rail and studied the water.

Tom flicked on a lantern and sat by the rail, dangling his legs off the side.

I did the same.

The black water of the lake lapped below our feet.

"So?" I shoved my hands into my pockets. "What did you want to tell me?"

Tom turned toward me. "Last night, y-y-you mentioned you were going to Mayo's b-b-birthday party."

"What about it?"

"Mayo's going to be thirteen, right?"

"Yeah, why?"

Tom stared ahead of him. "Then it's j-j-just like I thought. She's going to w-w-want you to take the Dare with her on her birthday."

"The Dare?"

"Yeah, s-s-spending the night in Foster's Woods. Every g-g-girl here does it when she turns thirteen. It's like a rite of p-p-passage or something."

"Spending the night in the woods?" I said. "If you haven't noticed, I'm doing that already. My house is right in the middle of a forest."

"No, I m-m-mean outside."

I wrinkled my face. "Like camping?" If that's all it took to make some pals, I was so there. "I don't get it. What's the big deal?"

"Paris," Tom began, "someone disappeared t-t-taking the Dare."

"Excuse me?" I said.

"Later th-th-they found her body in the woods."

I eyed him suspiciously. "Is this a joke?"

Tom shook his head. "Her name was B-B-Beth Conlon."

"So let me guess, when they found her body, it was all hacked into pieces?"

"No," Tom said. "Nothing like th-th-that. At least I d-d-don't think so."

"But this had to have happened a long time ago, right?" These kinds of stories always happened a long time ago. Like the one about the guy with the hook.

"She d-d-died before we were born," Tom confirmed. "In the eighties."

I knew it! This had to be made up. Instantly I was relieved, but Tom looked like he wasn't finished. "What?" I said.

"Your parents bought the property where the girl lived—where she d-d-died."

"What?!"

"Y-Y-Your land had been vacant for twenty years."

Suddenly, this tale sounded real. Now that I was a part of it.

"After it happened—"

"Wait. Hang on."

I had to think this over.

A girl takes a dare.

She spends a night in the woods where I live.

Then she dies.

. . . and . . .

My parents are the dumbest people here.

Oh, man.

"You want me to go on?" Tom asked.

I wasn't sure, but I nodded anyway.

"After she was found, everyone w-w-wanted to know how she died. But the sheriff didn't have any answers. At least n-n-nothing conclusive. Some people on this side of the lake moved, thinking there might be a m-m-murderer around."

I swallowed. *Murderer?*

Tom picked up a pebble. "Some even b-b-believed Beth's ghost haunted the woods." He tossed the rock into the water.

Ghosts? I shuddered. *No, Paris, calm down. You don't believe in ghosts.*

"Of course, there are others who j-j-just want to believe she died by accident."

"Accident? Like how?"

"Since her remains were f-f-found in a dried-up creek, they think she m-m-might have drowned."

I sighed in relief. "Well, that could have been it, right?"

"Yeah, but that d-d-doesn't explain everything."

"What do you mean?"

"A couple of years ago, Brianna D-D-Durbin took the Dare and couldn't talk for days afterward."

"What happened to her?"

He shrugged. "I'm not sure. The Durbins m-m-moved right after. But . . ." He paused, like he didn't want to say any more.

"But what?"

"But I think . . ." He leaned in. "Well, I think she might have run into the k-k-killer and somehow g-g-got away."

"For real?" I said. "So you believe Beth was murdered?"

"Maybe."

Still, a part of me found that hard to swallow. "Has anyone else been found dead in the woods since?"

"N-N-Not that I know of."

"Then there's probably no killer. Otherwise, wouldn't more bodies have piled up if everyone's been doing the Dare?"

Tom shook his head. "Paris, you've g-g-got to under-stand the mind of a killer."

"What do you mean?"

"Psychopaths d-d-don't always kill their victims one after another. From what I've read, there's usually a cool-ing off p-p-period. That time frame could be d-d-days or years. It's one of the reasons the best killers are so hard to c-c-catch. And who knows if Beth was even the f-f-first. There could be other victims n-n-no one has found yet."

"No way," I said, "a serial killer?"

"You c-c-can't rule that out."

I thought about it some more. "Okay, so why do you know all this stuff about murderers?"

"That's easy," Tom said. "I'd like to b-b-be a criminal investigator one day."

Great. It was just my luck that one of the first people I meet in Sugar Lake is into death and serial killers. Where were the normal people around here?

"Look, I d-d-don't want to scare you, Paris. Maybe th-th-the girl did drown. I just thought you sh-sh-should know."

I blew out a breath and tried to organize my thoughts. I wasn't used to getting this kind of news, and I didn't even know what to do with the information. Then as I looked at Tom, something else started to bug me.

"Tom, why are you telling me this? I mean, why do you even care?" I wondered if he was in on some cruel prank with Jay. Pull a fast one on the new girl.

"I d-d-don't see why I shouldn't tell you. Do you?"

I stared at him. Something about the way he was looking at me told me he was being sincere—about dead people and murderers. It was almost sweet. "No, I guess not."

"Plus," Tom added, "they s-s-say seventy-two percent of serial killers commit th-th-their crimes in the same vicinity as previous victims."

Terrific. "Thanks for the tip."

We both got quiet.

"Paris?" Tom said. "You all right?"

I tucked a loose strand of hair into my ponytail. "Yeah, I'm fine."

Tom didn't seem convinced. "You wanna g-g-go home?" he asked.

I nodded, even though going back there wasn't my first choice.

We walked out our bikes and rode across the dock. The sky was orange-purple now. It wouldn't be long before night fell. When we hit the road, I glanced at the bare trees around us. *You live where that girl did.*

Uneasiness settled inside me.

Where she died.

I pictured a dark figure, waiting in the woods. The hair on my arms bristled.

Tom slowed near the bait shop. The lights were off, and the sign read *Closed.* He looked up the road leading to my place. "You want me to ride with you?"

I stared at the trees and tried to make up my mind.

My silence seemed to answer for me.

"I'll go with you," Tom said. "Come on."

● ● ●

When I got home, I went straight to my personal library to see what I had on murderers. The only book I could find that might have something was my *Psychology Today* book. The words *murderers* and *killers* weren't in the index, but *crime* was. I turned to the page. The section was titled "Antisocial Personality Disorder."

A condition characterized by behavior that manipulates, exploits, or violates the rights of others. This behavior often results in crimes such as stealing, destroying property, and the killing of animals and humans.

I looked at Go, worried for her safety and mine.

The disorder typically presents itself in childhood. Children who flagrantly manipulate others, lie, and engage in activities such as fire setting and animal abuse are often later diagnosed with this condition.

I heard the garage door go up. Mom was home. I quickly scanned through the rest of the material, but nothing scared me more than what I had already read. I set the book down, ready to throw my mother on the Paris Pan grill for a nice chitchat about the property she bought. But my sister got to her first.

Verona's voice cut through the air. "Mom!"

I poked my head out of my room and listened.

"How could you sign me up for basketball without asking?"

"What, Wa-wa?" Mom said. Though I must live with the nickname Baby, Verona is cursed with Wa-wa, which means Doll. As in Barbie, as in American Girl, as in . . . Strawberry Shortcake. "Basketball is requirement. Athens take you home from practice."

"But what about *him*?" Verona said. "He said *he* doesn't have basketball."

"Your brother have asthma," Mom replied. "You have asthma, too, now? Too late. I sign letter. No choice."

"*No choice?* You're not in China anymore, Mother." Verona stomped toward the hall. "Just butt out!" Oh, my sister was angry. When she got mad, she became a geography expert, and Mom was "Mother."

"Wa-wa!" my mother shouted.

Bang! Verona slammed her door so hard, my books shook in their shelves.

I counted to three. Now it was my turn. I made a beeline for Mom.

She was still in the foyer, coat on and everything. She put her hand up. "You play basketball. That's it."

"That's not what I want to talk to you about," I said. "Did you know someone died here?"

She set down her purse. "Wha? Where?"

"Here! Beth Conlon, on our property!"

Mom sighed. "Oh, that." She took off her coat and shoes. "Why you think we get good deal?"

She knew?! I followed her through the living room. "Mom, did you hear me? A girl died. D-I-E-D."

"Make no difference." She stationed herself behind her paperwork in the dining room.

"But there could be a killer." I pointed at the sliding door. "Right outside!"

Mom flipped through a stack of bills. "Dead girl drowned."

"That's what you think," I said back.

She stopped to look at me, *hard*. "You think I buy land where girl murdered? You think your mother stupid?"

I didn't say anything.

"Answer!"

"No," I mumbled.

"Good." Mom cracked open her ledger. "Bank sign papers. Twenty acres ours." She flipped on the TV.

I huffed, then spun on my heels. Mom just didn't get it. Not about living here on a dead girl's property. Not about Mayo's birthday gift. Not about ANYTHING!

I got to my room, wondering when exactly she stopped caring about me.

Bang! I slammed the door with as much gusto as my sister.

chapter 5

After school the next day, Mayo, Dana, and I headed to the high school for my first basketball practice.

"You ready for the big party tomorrow?" Mayo said as we crossed the street.

I stared ahead. *Is that the one where we wind up on the back of milk cartons and then in the morgue?* "Yeah."

"Good," Mayo said. "Daddy's gonna run us by the shop beforehand to pick up candy."

"How much do we get to spend?" Dana asked as we approached the building.

"Twenty bucks on anything we want." Mayo opened one of the entrance doors. "And by the way, Paris, don't forget to bring—"

"I know. My flashlight." I followed my friends inside.

"No, Paris." Mayo glanced at Dana. *"Shh-shh-shh,"* they chanted. "FREAK repellent!" They broke up laughing.

"We are so mature," Mayo said.

I squinted at them. "Huh?"

"Robin," Mayo explained. "Her parents own the store. She lives there."

"Oh," I said.

But all I could think was, *Who lives in a candy shop?*

When Mayo flung open the girls' locker room door, I grimaced as the smell of sweat, deodorant, and stinky feet filled the air. Verona and her gaggle of friends were already there, huddled around a bench, gossiping about boys. She didn't seem to care that I had arrived, which was fine by me.

Gym clothes came out of lockers.

I stared at my jeans. "Maybe my first day will be spent watching."

Dana pulled on a T-shirt. "I wouldn't count on that."

Coach Dobson strutted in and blew her whistle. "Bumblebees, hurry up. We've got lots to do today." She tossed uniforms at Verona and me. "Wear the loaners, girls."

"See?" Dana said.

I put on the yellow and black outfit. *Ugh.* I looked like a school bus.

We headed out to the gym. Coach Dobson stood at the center of the court and blew her whistle again. "Let's move it!"

I took a spot in line between Mayo and Dana while Verona stood with her clone friends. I checked out the gym. Now I understood why the high school looked like a run-down warehouse. Half the building was a state-of-the-art basketball court, complete with digital scoreboards, bleachers, and a concession stand worthy of a thirty-screen movie theater.

The coach stood next to a cart filled with basketballs.

She grabbed a ball and paced the line, dribbling as she talked. "Honeys . . ." *Bounce, bounce.* "We've got new blood on the team." *Bounce, bounce.* She stopped in front of Verona. "Perhaps the Pans can save the girls' season." *Bounce.*

The coach ran backward and threw the ball at my sister.

With lightning-quick reflexes, Verona stepped to the side, and the ball slammed into the wall. "I'm supposed to catch that?"

Coach Dobson grunted and pointed her whistle at me. "Paris, show your sister how it's done."

Another ball flew through the air. My arms reached out like I was about to hug a pumpkin. *Bam!* It hit my body full force. I doubled over. A few of the girls giggled.

"You all right?" Dana whispered.

"Yeah, great," I managed.

"Bumblebees!" the coach barked. "What is the ball?"

"The ball is our friend!" the team chorused.

"And what do we do with it?"

"We dribble, we pass, we shoot, we score! Booyah!"

No way. Coach Dobson was a marine. Verona and I were in trouble.

But so was the coach. By the look on Verona's face, basketball would be an all-out war.

The rest of practice, my sister played horribly on purpose, citing every common illness in the book. She dribbled with her thumbs—carpal tunnel syndrome. She passed only if her teammate was a foot way—a nasty bout of arthritis. And when she shot, the ball only made it as high as her forehead—chronic back pain.

By the end of practice, Coach Dobson was ready to hang Verona from the hoop. I fared better. I dribbled like a baby chimp, but I was still a cut above the fifth graders.

"We *are* gonna get whupped," Dana said.

"I know who the real star of the Bumblebees is," Mayo added. "It's that sister of yours, Paris. *Princess Pan*."

I glanced at Mayo. *Princess Pan?* I couldn't have said it better myself.

● ● ●

Athens brought us home from practice, and as my siblings went to their rooms, I headed for the kitchen. With any luck, there might be a frozen burrito or two I could heat up. I opened the freezer, and boxes of orange Creamsicles greeted me. Forget the burritos. These must have been on sale this week. *Mom does love me.*

I got myself a Creamsicle, then noticed the blinking light on the answering machine.

I hit Play.

"Children, it's Mom. I be home late."

What's new?

Beep.

"Baby? . . ."

It was Daddy. I smiled, knowing he would talk to the machine for hours. Always amusing. "Wa-wa? . . . How's school? . . . Good, good. Athens? . . . School okay, too? . . . Good, good . . ."

As I listened to my father ramble, I started missing him. Maybe I should call him and tell him how I feel about living here. Maybe *Daddy* would understand. I picked up the phone, then something dawned on me. This was his fault, too, wasn't it? It's not like Mom bought this land on her own. If anything, he was the one who picked it out.

I listened to my father's voice go on. ". . . Your daddy working hard . . ."

I put the phone back down and narrowed my eyes.

"Yes, project not like I plan . . ."

Maybe he's building over a graveyard this time.

"But we do best we can, right?" Daddy laughed. "Okay, yes, yes. I miss you, too. Be home Sunday. That's right. One . . . two . . . three days from now. Bye-bye!"

I hit Delete just as Go padded in.

She headed to the patio door and whined.

Aw, man. I went to her and peered through the glass— at the darkening sky, the shadowy trees, and that stupid shed right in the middle of it. I thought about what Tom had said.

"Go, can't you hold it?" I said. *Like forever?*

She pawed the door.

"All right, all right." I let Go out, but I stayed close to the house and left the door open in case I needed to dive back inside. I didn't feel like dying today. That was tomorrow. *Stop it, Paris. You're being dramatic.* Then I remembered what Tom had said about that girl who couldn't talk for days after she did the Dare. My throat went dry. *Never mind. You should be freaked out of your mind.*

chapter 6

I spent the next day in class, trying to think of excuses for not doing the Dare. It wasn't until basketball practice that I was finally able to put it out of my mind. Two hard passes to the chest, a near strike to the head, and one face-plant in an attempt to shoot a layup can do that to a person.

After practice, Mayo, Dana, and I sat on a bench outside the gym, waiting for Mayo's dad to pick us up. I sighed as I watched Athens drive off with Verona. For the first time in my life, I wished I was with them.

"Hey, Mayo!"

Jay and Tom were walking toward us. "You watching us practice today?" Jay slung a gym bag over his shoulder. "See some real players in action?"

"Does it look like we are?" Mayo snapped. "Move out of the way. Your big head is blocking my view of the road."

I yawned and made a point of not looking at Tom.

"You heard Mayo," Dana said. "You'd think on her birthday she could get what she wanted."

Mayo glared at her. "Dana!"

"Ooh, a birthday?" Jay said. "So what are the plans for this happy occasion?"

"M-M-Mayo," Tom cut in, "you're not t-t-taking the Dare, are you?"

My jaw tensed. That was hardly subtle.

But Dana's gasp was all anyone needed to hear to know we were. *Great.*

"Maybe you need us along for protection," Jay said.

Mayo stood up. She had at least two inches on him. "The only one who needs protecting is you. Now move it."

"Come on, Jay." Tom pushed him along. "We're gonna be l-l-late." He glanced back at me as if to say, *I can't believe you're going to the party after what I told you.*

I stared at my shoes. Tom just didn't understand. He already had his own friends; I was only trying to make mine.

"That's Daddy," Mayo said as a truck came toward us. "Let's go."

We ran to the curb and threw our backpacks in the back of the red pickup. Mayo opened the passenger door, and a large man with a balding head and a shaggy beard was sitting behind the wheel. Mayo slid into the spot behind the gearshift, Dana got in next, and I closed the door.

"Hey, hey, birthday girl." Mr. Seaver put an arm around Mayo. "Dana, good to see you as always. And you"—he grinned at me—"you must be Paris."

I smiled. "Yes, sir."

Mr. Seaver jerked the stick shift, and the truck rumbled down the road. "Now, who's ready for candy?"

"I could use a Tootsie Pop right now," Mayo said.

"Jolly Ranchers all the way," Dana replied.

"Pop Rocks?" I hoped that sounded cool enough.

"Good one, Paris," Mayo said.

I smiled, peered into the darkness, and noticed our route to the shop looked familiar. It was almost as if Mayo's dad was taking me straight home. Eventually, we pulled up to Johnny's Bait and Tackle, and I stared at the white frame house, wondering what fishing had to do with candy.

"Don't take too long, ladies." Mr. Seaver gave Mayo a twenty-dollar bill.

The candy was here? At a bait and tackle shop?

We got out of the truck and Mayo shut the door. "First a precautionary measure." She whipped out her imaginary spray can. *"Shh-shh-shh!"* She sprayed herself, Dana, and me. "Don't let the freak get too close!" Mayo and Dana giggled.

I glanced at Johnny's. Then up the slope where I lived.

No way. Robin was my neighbor?

I decided I wouldn't tell my friends. I could be deemed a freak by association.

Mayo opened the door. A blast of warm air greeted us, and a bell jingled our grand entrance. Refrigerator cases labeled *BAIT* lined one wall of the room, and racks of candy lined another. A small dog came running toward us. "Fritz," Mayo said, "don't you dare jump on me." The dog barked and spun circles by her feet.

"Well, look who's here!" said a round woman standing

behind the counter. She studied me as she wiped her hands on an apron. "Mayo, you brought my neighbor to the hottest spot in Sugar Lake."

I froze by the door.

Mayo and Dana turned to stare at me. They didn't say anything, but I could tell they were making the connection, too. I had gone from the In girl to the Out girl in two seconds flat.

"Your father stopped by to introduce himself when you moved in," the woman continued. "I'm Mrs. Laney. Now, are you Paris or Verona? What unique names!"

"Paris," I mumbled.

Mrs. Laney pulled a Hershey's bar off a rack. "Well, Paris, give this to your dad. He about cleaned me out when he was here. This one's on me. Mayo, I got your favorites back in." She pointed to a rack of every flavor of Tootsie Pop imaginable.

"You are the best, Mrs. Laney," Mayo said. "Could I have a basket? We're buying a ton."

"Of course." She handed Mayo a plastic bin. "If it weren't for you kids, I couldn't stay in business all winter."

Mayo pulled me toward the rack. "Let's pick out our candy, Paris."

Wait a second. I was still in?

"Mrs. Laney," Mayo said, "do you have any Twizzlers?"

"I think we do," Mrs. Laney said. "I'll check the back. Fritz, come!" She lifted a curtain behind her.

Mayo and Dana huddled around me.

"Paris," Mayo whispered, "you didn't move onto the Conlon property, did you?"

I scrunched my face like I had no idea what she was talking about. "Who?"

Mayo pointed in the direction of my house. "The huge lot where the road ends."

I didn't say anything.

"This is incredible!" Mayo smiled. "This whole time I thought you'd moved into the old Mills place in town."

"So did I," Dana said, eyes wide.

I couldn't believe it. Were they happy my place was a crime scene?

The door jingled, interrupting their big discovery. We all turned.

It was Robin. She was wearing a navy coat and carrying a load of books in her arms. She paused at the doorway when she saw us.

"Hi, Robin," Mayo said in a singsong voice.

Robin didn't respond.

"Well, aren't you gonna say hi back?" Mayo stared at her for a few seconds, then a solitary word rolled out of her mouth. *"Freak."*

I winced. Robin didn't even blink.

I heard footsteps from the back of the house and Mrs. Laney mumbling to herself. She appeared from behind the curtain, a box of Twizzlers in her hands. "I knew we had some." She looked up and saw her daughter. "Honey, you're letting the cold air in! Come greet our customers properly." She dropped the box on the counter and pulled

Robin inside. The door jingled closed. "Go on. Don't be rude. Say hello."

Robin didn't move.

"If you keep this up," Mrs. Laney continued, "how are you gonna be friends with nice girls like these?" She took Robin's books and steered her to the register. "Check them out while I start dinner." She winked at us before she pushed past the curtain.

Without looking at us, Robin started ringing up items.

"That one costs a quarter," Mayo said in a school-teacher voice. "Drop it in the bag, Robin. And another quarter. That's a dime . . ."

Robin's fingers shook as she reached for each piece. I glanced at Dana to see if this was bothering her as much as it did me. But she was just standing there, watching, like this was a show she saw every day.

"Oops, Robin. You dropped that one. Now pick it up. Good . . . That's a quarter again . . ." When the last item was rung up, Mayo said, "Well, how much?" She slapped the counter. "Go on. Tell us."

Robin's lip trembled.

I had to do something. I tore the receipt from the register. "Nineteen dollars and eighty-five cents."

Mayo looked at me sideways, then dug into her pocket. She tossed the twenty at Robin. "Keep the change. Come on, girls."

Dana followed Mayo out of the shop. I started to leave but pretended to tie my shoes instead. When I got up, I glanced at Robin and opened my mouth. I wanted to tell her I was sorry about Mayo's behavior. I wanted to tell her that no one should be treated like that. But nothing came out. It was like the scene with Tom in the woods was replaying itself. *What is wrong with me?* Robin only stared back.

I bolted out of there.

Outside, Mayo and Dana giggled on the steps. "Did you see that?" Mayo said. "I think she was crying. Hey, Paris, what's your deal? You almost spoiled the fun in there."

I shrugged. "I was . . ."

I was what? Trying to go behind your back and make friends with the Freak? Go ahead, Paris. Say that. You'll just be as alone as Robin is.

"I was getting impatient," I told her. "How long does it take to buy something in there? Don't we have a party to go to? Jeez."

Mayo grinned. "Yes, we do, Paris." She slung an arm around me. "And I've got an idea for it that I'm sure you'll love."

That idea turned out to be the worst thing I'd ever heard.

chapter 7

We all piled into the truck, and Mayo's dad drove to the opposite end of town. It was a little different here compared to where I lived. Instead of being completely surrounded by Foster's Woods, the trees only lined one side of the road. On the other side, barren fields stretched across the evening landscape. Mr. Seaver slowed down and pulled to the right. A dirt road lay ahead of us, and we passed a gate with a sign marked *Abe's RV Park, travelers and permanent residents welcome!* As we went by trailer after trailer, the flickering lights of TVs glowed from windows, and old toys and dirty shoes littered doorsteps. It was hard to believe whole families lived inside these places.

Mr. Seaver parked in front of the last mobile home in the row. It seemed Mayo and I had something in common. She lived right up against the woods, too. *Terrific.* We got out, grabbed our things, and climbed a few steps to Mayo's trailer.

Mr. Seaver unlocked a dusty metal door. "Prepare to be surprised!" He waved us in.

"Wow!" Mayo said. Dana and I stepped in behind her. We dropped our stuff and gawked at everything: the zillion wooden horses standing in every blank spot in the room, a Gino's pizza box resting on a small Formica counter, and the frosted cake inscribed with *Happy 13th Birthday, Sweetcakes!*

"Mr. Seaver," Dana said, "this is great!"

"Thanks, Daddy." Mayo bear-hugged the man. "This is just like I wanted."

"Anything for my girl." Mr. Seaver cupped a hand to his mouth. "Roxy!"

He took off his coat and grabbed a jacket by the door. When he slipped it on, I read the word *SECURITY* stitched across the back. "ROXY!"

A door at one end of the room slid open and a girl with spiky black and blond hair and everything pierced popped her head out. "What?"

"Make sure your little sister doesn't set the place on fire," Mr. Seaver said. "Remember, you're in charge of three human lives here. And be nice, it's her birthday."

"Yeah, Dad, whatever." She slid her door closed.

"Mayo, one more hug for your daddy." He held out his arms. "Wish for something nice when you blow out your candles."

Mayo obliged. "I'll be wishing you hurry home."

Ugh.

Mayo's dad grabbed his keys, and then I remembered something. "Mr. Seaver?" I got my Mom's Polaroid camera out of my backpack. "Could you get a picture of us before you go?"

"Good thinking, Paris," Mayo said.

"I'd be happy to. Why don't you all stand by the cake?"

We arranged ourselves in front of the kitchen counter.

"One . . . two . . . three . . . Say cheese."

"Cheese!"

Mayo's dad pressed the button and a picture slid out. He laid it on the counter and handed the camera back to me.

"Thanks, Mr. Seaver." I watched the photo take shape.

"Anytime." He opened the door. "Have fun, girls."

After Mr. Seaver left, Mayo and Dana joined me in staring at the picture.

"I wonder how this Polaroid stuff works," Mayo said.

"Me, too," Dana said. "It's like magic or something."

"Yeah," I agreed, watching our smiling faces appear in front of me. "It *is* like magic." I stole glances at Mayo and Dana, and I couldn't believe I was standing here with not one, but *two* friends.

"Mayo!"

I turned. Roxy was sticking her head out into the hallway again. "Is Dad gone?"

I gaped at the heavy shadow circling Roxy's eyes, her lips black as tar. What had she done to herself?

I heard the truck peel away outside.

"Yup," Mayo said. "He's gone."

Roxy stepped into full view. She was dressed in a Led Zeppelin concert T-shirt and jeans that looked like they'd been through a thresher. "If you go out, make sure you get back before Dad comes home." She threw on a beat-up leather jacket. "Remember the deal?"

"I know, I know," Mayo said. "I won't tell him about your groping session with Ty tonight. Now where's my hush money?"

Roxy walked over to us, and I got a whiff of her luxury perfume—cigarette smoke.

"Don't spend it all in one place." Roxy slapped a five into Mayo's palm, then made her exit. She slammed the door so hard a palomino by the window fell on its side.

Mayo tucked the money into her pocket, then propped the horse back up. "All right, guys. We're having dessert first." She opened a kitchen drawer and pulled out a box of candles and a flashlight. *What was that for?* "Paris, grab the paper plates and utensils. Dana, get the cake."

Mayo went to a bench and released a latch against the wall. A diner-style table came down. I helped Dana stick candles in the cake and light them.

We sat on the bench with Mayo in the middle and sang the birthday song. Mayo took a deep breath and blew out her candles.

"It's official," she said. "I'm thirteen. Now let's get down to business." She plucked the candles out, then started working a knife down the cake. "Paris," Mayo said, "how much do you know about the Dare?"

I put on a blank face. "The Dare? Nothing." I hoped I looked convincing. Mayo passed me a slice.

"I figured. The Dare is a bad word around here. People never say it." She served another slice to Dana.

"They don't want kids doing it," Dana said.

"Parents." Mayo slid the rest of the cake toward her, then glanced at me. "Well, aren't you going to ask me what the Dare is?"

I played along. "What is it?"

Mayo smiled. She dipped her finger in the frosting and sucked her finger. "It's time, Dana. Hit the lights."

"But we haven't eaten our cake yet," Dana said.

"Dana."

"All right." Dana reached over and flipped the switch. For a moment, we sat in the dark, then suddenly, Mayo flicked on the flashlight. She pointed it up to her face. Shadows pulled at the corners of her nose and mouth.

"Way back in the eighties," she began, "there lived a girl named Beth, and some boy in her class told her that guys were better than girls. Of course, Beth thought he had it totally backward. That's when the dares started."

Then she died. The end.

But Mayo kept going.

"They took turns, putting each other up to dumb stuff like eating bugs and playing stupid pranks on the teacher. But with each turn, the stakes got higher. Until finally, the boy dared Beth to spend a night on her thirteenth birthday in Foster's Woods."

I rubbed my arms. Was the room getting colder?

"She left her house with only a flashlight in her hand and a sleeping bag on her back—"

"Hold up, Mayo," Dana interrupted. "Wasn't it a quilt?"

"No, Dana, it was a sleeping bag," Mayo said.

"Are you sure? Because the last time I heard the story, I thought it was a quilt."

"No, Dana, it was a *sleeping bag.* Who's telling the story here? Me or you?"

"Sorry, I was just trying to help."

"Like I was saying," Mayo said, "Beth left with only a flashlight and a sleeping bag. It was a rainy night—"

"No," Dana said, "it was snowing."

"Dana, what did I say?"

"Sorry! I can't help it!"

I looked at both of them and wondered how much of this whole thing was made up.

"Well, if you just let me finish, Dana," Mayo said, "we can worry about the details later. Now where was I?" She looked toward the ceiling. "That's right. Beth had a flashlight, a sleeping bag, and it was raining. She said goodbye to the boy and walked into the woods . . ."

Mayo took a deep breath for effect. *"She never came back."*

I tried to sound as surprised as possible. "She didn't?"

"Nope." Mayo leaned in. "Her folks reported her missing. A search party was put together, but they came up with nothing. It was raining so hard, dogs were no use, and when the skies finally cleared, there still wasn't any sign of her. Eventually, Beth's parents gave up looking. But a couple of years later, a hunter stumbled upon body parts in the woods—"

"Parts?" I said. Now wait a second. That's not what Tom had said. He said it was a body.

"Yup, parts," Mayo replied.

"Beth was only identifiable by her dental records," Dana added.

"Her eyes were all rotted out," Mayo said. "There wasn't much to examine, really. After all, they had only found *some* of her remains. So the coroner declared the reason for her death unknown. Some say the search party missed her and she decomposed from the elements. Maybe wild animals had gotten to her . . ."

This was worse than I'd thought.

". . . Others think she was murdered, chopped to bits, then scattered around the woods. On the property where she had lived." Mayo smiled. "That would be the Conlon property, Paris. Or should I say, *your* property."

"Are you freaked, Paris?" Dana said.

I was surprised she hadn't noticed my eyes watering. "What?" I took in a slow breath. *Be calm, Paris. Mayo and Dana have to be exaggerating.*

"You live where Beth probably died," Mayo said.

Right. "So?" I tried to play it cool. "What's freaky about that?"

Mayo slapped me on the back. "Dang, Paris! I knew I liked you the moment I saw you."

"You've got nerves of steel," Dana said. "Hey, Mayo, see how she acts when you tell her about the—"

There was more?

Mayo put her hand up. "I was getting to that, Dana. *Chill.*"

"Every now and then, guess what they find in the woods?"

I wasn't sure I was ready to hear this.

This time Mayo didn't wait for an answer.

"Dolls . . ." She let the word take over the room. "Lying on their backs . . ."

"Shiny, porcelain faces gazing skyward," Mayo and Dana said together.

Dolls?! Goose bumps marched up my arms.

Now, this part had to be made up. "No way. That can't be true."

"Yes way, it is true. Beth had a collection of them." Mayo gestured at the dark with the flashlight. "Like my horses. Legend has it the boy who dared Beth felt sorry for what he'd done. Or . . . the person laying out the dolls is the killer himself. *Or . . .* maybe it's the ghost of Beth telling us she's still around . . ."

"But . . ." I was about to say, "Tom didn't tell me any-thing about dolls," then quickly shut my mouth.

"But what, Paris?" Mayo said.

"But that's—that's crazy. Turn on the lights!"

"Yeah, that scared her, Mayo," Dana said. "The doll part is just creepy." She shivered.

"Um . . . lights?" I said again.

"Hang on, Paris. I'm not done." Mayo talked into her flashlight like it was a microphone. "Beth . . ." she intoned.

"Tonight, I am thirteen, and we will finish what you couldn't."

She turned the flashlight off.

"A rite of passage," Dana whispered in the dark.

"Cue the fluorescents," I said. *"Now."*

The lights came on. "So, Paris, what do you think?" Mayo said.

"Well, I . . . uh . . ." I raced through the excuses I'd made up earlier today. There was no way I was going out there now. "See, the thing is . . . we really shouldn't sleep outside tonight. I heard this morning there's a seventy percent chance of thunderstorms."

Mayo grinned. "Then that'll be perfect."

"Perfect?" I said.

"Why?" Dana asked.

"It'll make our night that much more authentic."

I held back a groan.

"Oh, Paris, you have nothing to worry about." Mayo picked up her fork. "We're not doing the Dare."

Dana and I stared at her. "We aren't?" we chimed.

"Not tonight. Now that we know Paris lives on the Conlon property, we can do it there. When she has us over." She stabbed the fork into the cake and took a bite.

"Excuse me?!" I said.

"That's my idea. Isn't it great?"

She's lost her mind.

"Don't you see?" Mayo said. "This is fate, Paris, *fate*! For weeks, Dana and I were planning on taking the Dare behind my house, miles from the sacred location. But now we have an opportunity to honor Beth's memory where it all happened."

"No way!" I said.

"Hear me out. I know what you're thinking. But plenty of people have taken the Dare and come out fine."

I immediately thought of the girl Tom had mentioned. "Is that so?"

"Well, there was that one incident," Dana said, offhand. "Hey, Mayo, you remember Bri?"

"Bri?" Mayo replied. "She was hazed. That's what Roxy told me."

"Hazed?" I said. "What do you mean?"

"Brianna was a new girl, like you, Paris. And Roxy thinks some of the girls she was with took the Dare too far. They probably made her do some crazy things just so she could be part of their clique. But Dana and I aren't like that."

Dana shook her head. "No, we're not."

"Look, Paris, you have nothing to worry about." She worked her fork into the cake again. "If a killer were still around, somebody else would have turned up dead by now. It was ages ago."

"That doesn't mean anything," I said, thinking of what Tom had told me. "Don't you know murderers go through a cooling period? Someone could strike again at any moment."

"Cooling period?" Mayo said. "Where did you learn that?"

I swallowed. "Um, no one. I mean, I just, uh . . . watched one of those shows on the Discovery Channel."

"Well, don't believe everything you see on TV. You are so missing the point."

Dana nodded. "Yes, you are."

"And that is?"

"Don't you get it? The three of us will bond!" Mayo set down her fork and pulled us in close. "In one night, we'll form a sisterhood that'll last a lifetime. Roxy said it was the best experience ever. How can you beat that?"

"Yeah, Paris," Dana said. "How can you?"

"And besides, if we don't do it," Mayo continued, "everyone is going to think we're wusses."

"Everyone?" I said. "Like who? Who would even care?"

"Well, we would, silly. Can you go on knowing you were too much of a fraidy cat to do the Dare? Every self-respecting girl in Sugar Lake does it. It's like Dana said, a rite of passage. So . . ." Mayo paused to stare at me hard. "Are you in or *out*?"

I looked at Mayo and Dana and my brain started arguing with itself.

Voice #1: Don't go along with it, Paris. Are you crazy?

Voice #2: Please. Mayo said plenty of girls have taken the Dare and come out fine. Why can't that be you?

I glanced at my backpack that had our photo in it. *Don't you want to fill up that album? Don't you deserve it after all these years?* I bit my lip. The answer was obvious.

"Well?" Mayo said.

"Fine."

"Then it's settled," Mayo replied. "Now, who wants a Coke?"

chapter 8

When I got home the next morning, Verona was sitting on the living room carpet, surrounded by receipts and invoices. *Great.* Every year, Mom recruited us to sort paperwork to prepare for income taxes. I quietly took off my shoes, dropped my backpack to the floor, and tried to make a quick exit to my bedroom.

"Mom! Baby's home," Verona said without looking up.

I glared at my sister.

My mother called from the dining room, "Baby, help Wa-wa!"

"Mom wants the bills sorted by date and category this time." Verona chucked a big stack of papers onto the floor. "That's your half."

I frowned at the stack of bills by my feet and plunked down next to her. As I went through the invoices, my mind quickly got to thinking about last night. I glanced at the patio door and wondered how Verona could be so clueless to the horror all around her. Maybe she didn't know about Beth. Maybe if I told her the story, we could unite as one and stage a Pan sister rebellion.

It could happen.

"You won't believe what I learned last night," I said casually.

Verona thumbed through a pile and pulled out a receipt. "Who cares what happened at your stupid party?"

"You'll care when it has everything to do with you." I placed an invoice onto a stack.

"Really, Paris," my sister said dryly. "Tell me. I'm dying to know."

I stopped sorting and lowered my voice. "Mayo gave me the complete 4-1-1 on this place we call home."

"Oh, you mean Beth?"

"You know?!"

"Yeah, I know." Verona placed a receipt onto another stack. "Jen told me as soon as I told her where I lived."

"And you aren't freaked out?"

"Why should I be? It happened a long time ago."

Hmm. Maybe Verona hadn't heard the same version of the story I had. "Not even the stuff about body parts and finding dolls in the woods?"

"Whatever!" My sister pulled out another receipt and dropped it into a pile. "I'm sure half of that stuff is made up by little kids—like you—just to freak each other out." She stopped to stare at me. "And it's working. Look at your face." She started laughing. "Scared, Paris? Shivering like a baby under your blankie at night?"

"No." Why had I even thought Verona would care? That girl was more clueless than my mother—hands down. I ignored my sister's snickers and continued through my stack of invoices. How come no one, besides me and Tom, was worried?

Weren't there plain facts that couldn't be disputed? Like, number one, someone disappeared on our property. Two, no one knows how the girl died. And three, not a single person has had the guts to live here until we came along.

I glanced at my sister, who was humming like she didn't have a care in the world.

Why shouldn't I be scared?

After I finished organizing the bills to Mom's satisfaction, I picked up my backpack and went to my room. At my desk, I pulled out my Snuffy pen and my school calendar. As much as I dreaded this, I had to set a date for the Dare— my friendships with Mayo and Dana depended on it. As I glanced at February, I thought about how long I could put it off. I decided about two weeks from now would be optimal—Saturday, the 20th. There was still plenty of time to think of a way out of it, and I could make up plenty of excuses for the date without Mayo thinking I was stalling.

I marked the day with a skull and crossbones. Then I grabbed my notebook and started planning for the worst-case scenario.

I imagined I was in the woods with Mayo and Dana. I had a flashlight as my only weapon and a sleeping bag for a shield. I'd need backup, more protection. I looked at Go sitting on the floor. She was too busy licking herself to protect anything.

Tom. I needed Tom. Of course.

I wrote him a note:

*A certain someone is convinced you-know-what
will be more "fun" at my house. I'm going to try to
get out of it, but in case all else fails, can you help?
I don't want you to stop me or anything (no telling
what could happen if a certain someone realized
we were talking). Just watch out for me if we go,
okay?*

I sketched a stick figure of me praying and hoped the
desperate drawing would tip the scale in my favor.

Then I added:

*Why didn't you say anything about the body parts
and dolls?*

I folded up the note and put it into my backpack for
Monday delivery. As I zipped up my bag, I caught a
glimpse of the picture from Mayo's party. I fished it out,
got my photo album from my bookshelf, and taped the
photo on the first available spot in the "Friends" section.
The question next to it read, *What do you and your
friends like to do together?*

Well, *like* was a questionable term. So far, I hadn't enjoyed doing much with Mayo and Dana other than hanging out at lunch, and even *that* was debatable. But still, I
didn't mind. I stared at our happy faces. Enjoying other
activities together would come in time. I decided I'd wait
to answer the question and returned the album to the
bookshelf.

Go started whining.

She was looking at the door. *Ugh, not again.*

I glanced at the window. At least the sun was out. Bad things never happened in broad daylight.

With Go following me, I headed to the patio door. "Mom, I'm taking Go out." Perhaps if she knew I was leaving, she'd notice if I didn't return. She mumbled something back. *Not.*

I hooked up Go and let her out. I avoided looking at the woods and studied the side of my house instead. "Go, you've got ten seconds." The leash started to spool out and I began counting. "One Mississippi, two Mississippi, three Mississippi . . ." When I was about to hit ten, the leash jerked in my hand. "Go?" I didn't see her. I tried to remain calm. The leash was probably caught on something. My gaze followed the leash into the trees, but I couldn't trace it. That's when I noticed the shed. I caught my breath.

The door was open a perfect terrier-sized width.

"Go, get back here now!"

She popped her head out.

I sighed with relief. "That's a good girl. Come out."

Ignoring me, she trotted right back into the building. "Oh no, you don't." I pulled on the leash, but it wouldn't give. *Terrific.* It *was* tangled on something. At least, that's what I told myself.

I closed my eyes and gathered my courage. *Just get her, Paris.* As I followed Go's leash through the woods, I tried not to think about killers and dead people and dolls.

When I was only about ten feet from the shed, I couldn't see the gap in the doorway from where I was standing. Just the door and Go's leash bending around it. I came across what the leash was tangled on—the base of a tree. I quickly circled the trunk, then gripped the leash handle. "Go, game's over!"

Nothing better come out of there but my dog.

I gave the leash a good tug, which made the shed door swing open. Suddenly, the leash felt incredibly light and I lost my balance. I landed on the ground as something flew through the air. The next thing I saw was Go's collar hanging from a branch. The leash was still connected to it . . . but Go wasn't.

I stared at the shed as a horrible feeling radiated from the pit of stomach. Did someone have Go?

"Paris, what are you doing?!"

I almost screamed before I realized it was my brother yelling at me. I glanced toward the house. Athens was stepping out onto the patio, wrangling on his jacket.

"Why is the shed open?" Athens said as he headed into the woods. "Is Go in there?" He noticed the collar hanging from the tree. "Without her leash?!" He broke into a dash and ran past me.

"But Athens!" I finally choked out as I scrambled to my feet. "Athens!"

"Oh my God!" my brother shouted.

I was about to shriek for help, but then I heard Athens say, "Go is dirtier than a pig!" He walked out of the shed with Go under his arm looking like she just had a mud bath.

No one was in there?

"Mom's going to be pissed," Athens muttered. "You're washing her, not me!"

My brother came over and brought down the collar from the tree branch. "And how did you get this up here?" He tossed it at my feet. "Bring it in."

My body began to relax as I reeled in the leash. As Athens headed back to the house, he muttered about how irresponsible I was for letting Go nearly dig her way to the earth's core. I started to follow my brother, then I looked back at the shed. *Wait a second.*

Go was digging in there?

The horrible feeling in my stomach came back. *Digging for what? Fingers? Toes?*

I sped up to catch up with my brother.

By the time I got to the patio, I'd talked myself down. She's a terrier; she digs. Mom had threatened more than once that Go be swapped for a bird because of her tendency to destroy the lawn. I let out a breath. This whole Dare thing was making me so paranoid.

I reached for the door.

"Wait, Paris," Athens said.

I turned. "What?"

"I want to ask you something."

The sudden nice tone of his voice caught me off guard. I became suspicious.

"Do you know anything about Roxy Seaver?" Athens said. "Her sister, Mayo, is in your grade."

I raised a brow. *Roxy?* He didn't like her, did he?

I stared at my dirty dog in Athens's arms. Maybe my knowledge about the girl would be useful. "Well, that depends," I said.

Sibling bartering was about to take place.

"What's your price?" he grumbled.

"Give Go a bath and take her out for . . . two weeks."

"Two weeks?" Athens reached for the door. "Forget it." He paused before he opened it. "Make it three days."

"Three days?! *No way.*"

"Four, then."

"Six," I said. "And that's my final offer. Going once . . ."

Athens looked down at Go.

"Going twice . . ."

"Fine. Spill it."

"Roxy makes out with Ty, and at night, she disguises herself as a mutant raccoon."

Athens frowned. "Ty, huh?"

"And she smokes," I added. "And her favorite color has to be black. Oh, and she's into leather, and she . . . uh . . . likes some band called Led Zeppelin."

"Jeez, Paris. Did you read her diary, too?"

"Nope, couldn't find it."

My brother tried to hold back a smile. I was surprised by this twisted expression on his face. It'd been so long since I'd seen him smile at anything. Then his smile vanished like he'd just remembered he wasn't supposed to like me. "Anything else?" he grumbled.

"Nope." I handed him Go's leash. "See you later."

That night, I went to bed, thinking about what had happened at the shed today. I pulled up the covers and glanced at the window. Then I nudged Go with my feet. "There wasn't anything scary in there, right?"

Go sighed as if to say, "No."

Satisfied, I turned on my side and called it a night.

I didn't know how long I'd been asleep when a sound startled me.

I sat up as Go's growl filled the darkness.

She was at the window, standing on her box. Moonlight shined against her fur. The wind whistled in. Why was the window open?

Go growled louder.

I scanned the room—only the shadows of branches swayed across the walls.

Tap, tap.

I glanced at the window again. I took in a breath.

Someone was standing outside now, a dark shape against the trees—the shape of a girl.

Go whined.

The girl raised a hand to the glass.

Tap, tap.

I was so scared, I could hardly breathe.

The girl turned slightly, and the moon revealed her face.

Her eyes were cool steel. Her hair was done in braids.

"Robin?" I whispered. The whistle of the wind became the sound of sobbing. "Robin, is that you?" The trees shook behind her.

Tap, tap.

I started to push back the covers, wondering what was wrong. Wondering if I could help.

Eeeeeeeer.

I froze.

That had to be the shed.

Go pawed the window.

Robin beckoned me to follow.

Then she didn't look like Robin anymore. She looked like someone I didn't know.

I squeezed my eyes shut. *You don't believe in ghosts.* I gripped my blankets.

Close the window, Paris!

My body refused to obey.

Then all of a sudden, I could see the shed in my mind. The open door waited.

My voice screamed in my head. *Close the window now! Bang!*

I woke up, breathless. I stared at my window. Moonlight shined in. No one was there.

Go groaned at my feet.

Relief came over me. *It was all just a dream.*

Yet it had felt so real. I quickly shook my head.

No, ghosts are about as real as Santa Claus and the tooth fairy.

I looked at the window again. Then I got a sinking feeling that something was wrong.

Hadn't I left my blinds *down*?

"Go, come," I whispered. She padded up my blanket.

I gathered up my dog and held her tight.

chapter 9

When the sun rose, I was still in bed with Go in my arms. All night I'd faded in and out of sleep. I couldn't shake the scariness of the dream, and I couldn't stop thinking about the shed, wondering if there was a link between that rotten building and Beth's untimely death. Tom's murder theory played at the back of my mind. Let's face it—the shed was a perfect hideout for a killer. It's dark, it's in the woods . . . Maybe he watched Beth's house from that wretched building, just waiting for the perfect moment to attack. He might have even killed Beth in there—

Someone knocked on my door.

"Baby?"

Daddy's voice snapped me from my gruesome thoughts. *When did he get home?*

"Time to get up," my father said. "I don't drive from Choctaw to stare at door."

I put Go down, jumped out of bed, and burst into the hallway. "Daddy!"

"Hey, Baby." My father looked down, wearing his favorite flannel work shirt—the one where the stripes always made him look rounder than he was. The familiar sight was almost enough to make me feel safe again.

He smiled. "You growing so fast."

I gave my father a ferocious hug. "I'm so glad you're here."

"Wow, wow, wow!" he said. "That's more like it."

"Daddy, there's something you've got to do." I took his hand and pulled him into my room.

"Baby, what's wrong?"

I pointed at the window. "Get rid of that!"

"Why?" my father said. "That's new double-paned Pella."

I rolled my eyes. "Not the window, the shed! IT HAS TO GO."

Daddy frowned. "Baby, is that how you speak to father?" He yelled for Mom. "Doro-see! What you teach Baby? Such angry girl."

I ignored my father's remark and kept my finger pointed in the direction of the shed. "Something isn't right about that thing. Last night, I had this dream—"

"What you say, Frank?" My mother walked in, her hair in a shower cap and a clean paint brush in her hand.

"Mom, you have to help me." I tugged her toward the window. "Make Daddy take down the shed. Now."

"Baby, stop!" Mom scolded.

"Doro-see?" my father said. "What you painting?"

"Who hasn't finished kitchen?" Mom complained.

"I told you. I do that later."

"Daddy—" I cut in.

My father paid no attention to me and kept talking to Mom. "I'm tired and want to spend day watching TV."

"I don't think so," she said.

I put my hands on my hips. "Helloooo!"

They turned to look at me. "What?"

"The shed!"

"Ay-yuh." Daddy ran a hand through his hair. "Your father is not taking a shed down today."

"Right," my mother agreed. "He paint today." She left my room.

"But the shed's a safety hazard!" I said.

"Well, Baby, watch where you go, okay?" My father patted my head, then went to the door. "Shed is dangerous."

My father left, and I realized how hopeless the situation was.

● ● ●

That evening, the entire family gathered at the table for dinner, the way we do when Daddy's home. I think this little tradition is how my parents like to pretend we're still a Pan family unit. Never mind my father will be leaving again tomorrow.

I stared at my bowl of broccoli-beef over rice porridge and pushed the stuff around with my chopsticks. Another little mealtime rule: you don't leave the table unless your bowl is clean. According to Mom, people were starving in Ethiopia. People were *always* starving in Ethiopia.

Daddy cleared his throat. "I tell you, this project got some big problems . . ."

Athens and Verona groaned from across the table.

Daddy loved to talk about his projects. Actually, Daddy just loved to talk.

"Foundation not even poured yet. My worker don't know what they do." He shook his head. "I go back tomorrow and watch them like bird."

"Hawk," I corrected.

"Right, hawk!" Daddy's chopsticks paused in the air. He glanced at my mother. "Why they say that? Hawk must have good eyes." He smiled at the revelation, then slurped from his bowl.

Mom didn't say anything. She laid another piece of broccoli into my dish on top of the pile she'd already built up. I gave my mother a dirty look.

"Doro-see," Daddy said, "got more beef?"

"Frank, you have enough," Mom scolded. "What doctor say? Too much meat. Too much junk food."

"Yes, yes." Daddy scooted back from the table. "High cholesterol, he say . . ." He went to the wok in the kitchen. ". . . High blood pressure. Everything, high." He helped himself to more. "That's doctor's job, dah-ling. Don't worry. When the Lord want to take me, he will."

More groans. We all knew Daddy's statement was the beginning of a long recounting of the many times he had tempted death—the time he almost fell off a roof, the time a backhoe missed him by inches, the time he nearly choked on a cheese stick. Athens and Verona shoveled rice into their mouths faster. They knew the sooner they finished, the sooner they could leave.

Daddy was on his last story now—the colonoscopy scare. When he finished, he popped a piece of meat into his mouth and said, "So . . . how's school?"

Athens didn't even glance up. "Great." He took his last bite and picked up his dishes. "I'm done."

Verona did the same. "Me, too."

Daddy watched them leave, then looked at Mom and me. My mother wearily shrugged, then took her own dishes to the kitchen.

"What, what I say?" Daddy said to me.

"Oh, nothing, Daddy." I drowned a floret of broccoli in my porridge, wanting to tell him about everything—the Dare, the shed, Mayo. But somehow I knew if I did, I was just living up to my nickname—Baby—and I was hardly that. Instead, I hoped he would drag it out of me. I took a deep breath and gave him the perfect lead-in. "School's *fine*." Every parent knows that when a child says *"fine,"* things are completely the opposite.

I looked up at my father and waited.

Daddy's face softened a little, and he leaned across the table. Hope rose in my chest.

He nudged my bowl. "You need help with that?"

I stared at him as something huge occurred to me.

Daddy had no clue about me anymore, did he? *Just like Mom.*

I pushed the bowl toward him. "Yes, Daddy, that's *fine*."

I left the table and went to my room. After I closed my

door, I just stood there, wanting to kick something. I tried to calm down. Maybe I should focus on something else instead, like my history homework. Perhaps something as dull as the Cold War would take my mind off my insensitive parents. As I grabbed my textbook from my backpack, the phone rang in the next room. *It never ended with Verona.*

I opened my book to a chapter when suddenly— *Bang!*—

Verona appeared at my door, holding her phone. "It's for you."

The information took a second to soak in. "Really?"

"Yeah," Verona said. "I didn't believe it, either."

She dropped the phone onto my bed. "You've got five minutes, and don't smear your dirty fingerprints all over my handset." She shut the door.

I picked up the phone and rubbed my hands all over it like it was a dishcloth. Then I sat on my bed, wondering who it could be. I got this tiny hope that it was Tom, calling to talk to me about the Dare. "Hello?"

"Hey, Paris!"

I bit my lip. "Hey, Mayo, what's up?" Though I knew I should have been happy to have someone call me for once, for *some* reason, the moment wasn't so joyous.

"Just wondering if you've figured out when we're going to have our next party. Have you talked to your parents yet?"

"Yeah," I lied.

"And?"

"Saturday, February twentieth. But Mom says *after* dinner." No sense in exposing my friends to my family any more than necessary.

"February twentieth? That's two weeks from now. You sure we can't do next weekend?"

"That's Presidents' Day weekend. We're going out of town to see my grandparents."

Never mind they were all in China.

"All right . . ." Mayo sounded disappointed. "I'll call Dana and see what she thinks. At least this will give us lots of time to plan."

"Plan?" I said. "What more is there to plan?"

"Look, Paris . . ." Mayo hushed her voice. "My dad's still here. I'll fill you in at school tomorrow. But don't worry. You're going to love my idea, I just know it. Later!"

I hung up.

Somehow, I doubted that.

chapter 10

The next morning, I waited for my sister to meet up with a bunch of her friends before school, then I split for the school yard. I dropped my note to Tom in the tree, then spent the morning trying to catch his eye to let him know about my special delivery. Eventually, Tom seemed to understand my raised eyebrows and occasional head jerks and he asked to be excused to go to the restroom. I relaxed.

At lunch, Mayo, Dana, and I sat on our steps. "So Paris," Mayo began, "Dana and I are on for the twentieth."

Dana nodded as she unwrapped her sandwich. "My mom said she could drive us to your place. But guess what, Paris? You'll miss Valentine's Day with us. Mayo and I always hang out and watch a movie together. Bake brownies and stuff. I was hoping you could come."

"For real?" I couldn't believe it. My friends finally suggest activities I'd enjoy, and I'll be "out of town." My shoulders sagged. "I guess you'll have to make do without me."

"Don't worry about it," Mayo said. "V-Day will be nothing compared to you-know-what." She straightened. "Especially now that I've got even *better* plans for it."

I inwardly groaned.

"Like what?" Dana said.

"I was thinking," Mayo replied, "we shouldn't just sleep anywhere on Paris's property."

"We shouldn't?" Dana and I said.

"Nooo. Check this out." Mayo pulled out a newspaper clipping from her lunch bag. I read the header: OBITUARIES.

"This gave me my latest idea," she said. "The *Gazette* has tons of stuff on dead people. We should read up on our little friend. Find out exactly where they found her."

"Why would we want to know that?" I asked. "I thought the deal was we spend the night and that's it. No history lesson required."

"Yeah, Mayo," Dana said.

"Don't you guys think if we do you-know-what, we should *really* do it on you-know-who's resting place? She'd want it that way, right? Imagine all that *symbolism*!"

Symbolism? That only happened in books and movies, not when you're lying on the ground in the woods where people have taken their last breaths! "Listen, Mayo, I don't need to do research to know where she went down. I have a feeling it's somewhere near where I sleep. So if you want to do you-know-what right, we spend the night in my room."

I hoped I could bait Mayo into bringing the party indoors.

A smile spread across her face. "Man, Paris, are you still scared from the birthday party?!" She laughed.

Dana nodded. "I think she is, Mayo. Maybe we shouldn't have told her the part about the dolls."

Great. Now both of them were laughing.

"Aw, Paris. Don't worry. Dana and I will be with you every step of the way. In fact, go with that fear. Let that fear feed the moment we step into the woods. It might bring us all closer together."

Oh, brother.

"You know, I didn't think I'd ever say this . . ." Mayo leaned in. "But tomorrow after practice, we're going to the library. It's the perfect place to look up stuff on the computer without people breathing down our necks. Tell your parents we're working on a science project. Dana, can your mom take us?"

"To the library?" Dana said. "She'd take us every day if that's what we wanted."

"Perfect," Mayo said.

"What's so p-p-perfect?"

I looked back. Tom was standing behind us. A part of me was relieved. I think my heart might have even jumped a little at the sight of him. Maybe he could find a way to save me.

"No one asked you, dimwit," Mayo said. "And since when did you start thinking you could invade our privacy?"

Tom didn't answer.

"Well, aren't you going to leave?"

He crossed his arms. "Not until you tell me what you all are talking about."

Did he always have to be so obvious?

Mayo stood. "You're lucky I'm not in the mood to break a knuckle on your thick skull today." She pushed past him. "Come on, girls."

Dana and I got up, but before I stepped inside the school, I gave Tom a look that meant, *What on earth was that?*

"What?" Tom mouthed.

As I walked inside, I wondered if involving Tom was a little too risky. If he wasn't careful, he could ruin it for me.

● ● ●

That evening, I sat at my desk in my pajamas and put together a note.

> *Thanks for trying to help at lunch. I really appreciate it. But could we try to be more subtle?*

I bit my lip. Hopefully these simple words would rein Tom in.

I continued writing.

> *So here's what I learned today. Mayo wants to do research on you-know-who, so I will spend tomorrow night at the library Googling a dead person. Yippee.*

We've also set Saturday, February 20, for you-know-what. My house. Keep your calendar open.
P.S. I am trying to get out of it, honest!

Bang! I jumped at the sound.

"Paris?" Verona said.

I closed my notebook and turned around. "What?"

My sister swooped in, wearing her new basketball uniform. *Verona style.* She'd knotted the jersey so her belly button showed and shored up the shorts so they functioned as hot pants. "What do you think?" She twirled in place.

"You'll get thrown off the team if you wear your uniform like that."

Verona smiled. "Thank you, Paris. That's all I wanted to know. Wednesday's game will be my first and last." She spun herself out of my room.

I got up, shut my door, and trudged back to my desk.

If the Dare didn't kill me, basketball would.

● ● ●

The next day, I yawned as I dropped my note in Robin's tree. Last night, I hadn't gotten much sleep. I heard a tap, tap, tapping against the house, and I was too scared to find out what it was. Needless to say, that was not the way to start the morning.

The end of the day wasn't much better. After practice,

Dana's mom took us to the library. When we got out of the car, I wondered what architect had closed his eyes and designed this place. The library looked like a box with only a couple of windows. Inside, Mayo stepped up to the circulation desk and signed up for some time at the computer. We passed some stacks and headed for the flickering monitor toward the back. Mayo pulled out a chair. "Take a seat, genius."

"Me?" I looked at the hardware, which was practically the size of Mayo's trailer. "You sure this can get to the Internet?"

"Positive. Roxy buys her eyeliner from this very machine."

That's odd. I thought her makeup came from a nearby tar factory. I reluctantly sat in front of the monitor, and Mayo and Dana pulled up two chairs.

I opened the browser, then typed in *Beth Conlon* and *Sugar Lake, Oklahoma.* I clicked the mouse and hoped for no results.

All three of us gasped.

"Eleven thousand, four hundred hits?!" I said.

The first one was a listing for Sugar Lake's chamber of commerce. Another was someone's MySpace page who happened to live here. A third was about a music company called Sugar Lake that wasn't even in Oklahoma.

"We must have done something wrong," Mayo said.

"Try adding quotes," Dana volunteered. "Around Beth's name and then around the city and state."

I glared at Dana. She wasn't helping. I did as instructed. Zero hits.

"Shoot," Mayo said. "Now what?"

"Ladies?"

I clicked off the window and looked back. The librarian was only a couple of feet away, peering over her spectacles. "It's getting loud here."

"Mrs. Reynolds," Mayo said innocently, "we can't find anything on our topic. Could you help?"

The librarian lit up like she'd never been asked this question before. She took off her glasses and placed them on her head. "What's your subject?"

"Science?" Dana said.

"The weather!" Mayo added. "We have to record daily temperatures in Sugar Lake during the 1980s and compare them to today's weather patterns. A comprehensive study on global warming."

I stared at Mayo. *Where the heck does she come up with this stuff?*

"What a topic," Mrs. Reynolds said. "You're not going to find that on the Web. Only the state's two largest papers are archived on the Internet, and neither go back that far. Besides, I don't believe they would have what you're looking for. Come with me."

We followed Mrs. Reynolds to an ancient microfiche station. "All the issues of the *Sugar Lake Gazette* are on microfilm." She held up a slide that was the size of a large index card. "Each one holds about five issues. Temperatures can usually be found on the front page." She demonstrated how the station worked and pointed to a beat-up copy machine attached to the station. "You can print from there. And remember, the library closes at 6:30 p.m. You've got an hour."

She walked away, and I studied the box of slides in front of me. You-know-who was in there . . . *somewhere.*

"Mayo, what year do we start with?" Dana whispered.

"Why don't we try 1985?" Mayo said. "That's when Roxy thought it was." She fished a film out of the box and slipped it under the slide plate. A headline appeared on the screen. *Grocer Closing after Half Century.* My eyes glazed over. *County Health Department to Get New Building . . .*

This could take forever.

"We're never going to find anything," Dana whispered.

"Don't worry, Dana." Mayo pushed the slide plate along. "We will soon enough. I'd swear it on my grave."

For the next fifty minutes, we sifted through Sugar Lake history one microfilm at a time, and we found nothing. The clock hit 6:30. "Time's up!" I announced.

"Shoot," Mayo said. "We're not even halfway through the year." She pushed the slide plate along.

"Come on, Mayo," Dana urged. "My mom's going to be outside any minute. We gotta go."

Yes!

We threw on our jackets and grabbed our backpacks.

As we passed the front desk, I noticed a girl sitting in a reading chair. I could only see the back of her head, but I saw the braids, and I knew it was Robin.

"Look," Dana whispered. "I bet she comes here every day."

"What do you expect?" Mayo said as we waited in the vestibule. "The Freak has no life."

"Um, Mayo," I replied. "Do I need to point out we're also here?"

"Oh, I think she's coming," Mayo said.

I glanced back.

Robin was getting out of her chair.

Mayo straightened like a rooster about to go into battle.

I prayed Robin wouldn't come this way.

She put on her coat and her backpack, then started for the doors. But as soon as she saw us, she veered toward a shelf, grabbed an armful of books, and hurried to the counter. *Smart girl.*

"My mom's here," Dana said.

"Come on, Mayo!" I held the door open.

"Aw, man," Mayo complained. But instead of following us out, she breathed on the glass, fogging it up. "I'll be right there." She dragged her finger through the fog, spelling out the first letters—*FR.*

I couldn't let her finish. "Mayo, Mrs. Reynolds will see you."

I pulled her out the door and looked over at Robin. She was staring right at me, and even though I'd done nothing wrong, a wave of guilt came over me.

● ● ●

When I got home, I was so exhausted, I skipped dinner and went right to bed. As I settled in for the night, I thought about seeing Robin at the library, then remembered how she'd appeared in my dream. I wondered if my subconscious was trying to work something out. I closed my eyes, wary of what my brain would conjure up next.

Of course, trying to go to bed without dinner hardly set me up for a restful night. I tossed and turned, and by midnight, I was so hungry, I had to drag myself out of bed.

I looked at Go. "Wait right here, girl."

I quietly opened the door and tiptoed down the dark hall to the kitchen. I grabbed an entire box of Creamsicles from the freezer and headed back to my room. But just as I closed my door, I heard giggling.

Go was licking her chops, too busy staring at my frozen treats to notice anything. She whined.

"Shhh!" I didn't move. I couldn't tell where the sound had come from. I concentrated on the window directly opposite me. No one was there. Branches outside glistened in the moonlight.

Eeeeeeeeeer.

I stared at the box of Creamsicles in my hands. *It's just low blood sugar, Paris. Low blood sugar.*

I heard the giggling again, then *bang!*

The shed.

I dropped the Creamsicles, flung open the door, and

raced down the hall. "Mom, Mom!" I got to her bedroom and flipped on the lights. "There's someone outside!"

My mother mumbled, "Wha, Wa-wa?"

"Mom, it's me, Baby. I heard someone." I pulled back her covers. "You have to check it out."

Mom slowly sat up. "What?"

"Moooomm," I moaned. "Hurry! The shed—someone's in the shed!"

My mother sighed and stuck out her hand. "Give me robe."

I dashed to the door, got it from the hook, and handed it to her.

"Shed?" Mom said. Suddenly, she sounded more awake. "Who's inside shed?"

"How am I supposed to know?!" I tugged on her until she was standing. "I heard her laughing. Get out there, Mom."

My mother put on her robe. "Her?!" She stopped. "Baby, what you playing?"

"Nothing, Mom, honest." *Would you hurry up?*

"Baby, I told you, dead girl DEAD." She shrugged off her robe and lay back down again.

"No, Mom. This is real. I heard someone, I swear."

Just then Verona shuffled in in her pajamas, hair a mess. "What's going on?"

"Did you hear it, Verona?" I said.

"The shed?" My sister yawned. "Yeah, someone needs to put a bolt on that thing. It opens and closes all the time."

"Wa-wa, Baby," Mom muttered, "let me sleep."

I ignored my mother. "No, not that, the giggling."

"Giggling?" Verona looked confused. "You heard a *girl* giggling?" Then she narrowed her eyes at me. "Yeah, Paris, there's a chick walking around at midnight in our yard. Ohmigod, are you seriously still thinking about Beth?" She turned to leave. "You heard Mom—go to bed."

Athens walked in, annoyed as ever. He tightened the belt on his robe. "Do any of you know what time it is? What's going on?"

"Paris thinks there's a *ghost* haunting our shed," Verona called as she headed back to her room.

"No, I don't!" I protested. "There's a girl outside."

"A girl? Paris, what are you on?" Athens shook his head as he left the room. "Give me a break."

"But . . ." Why wouldn't anyone listen to me?

"Baby?" Mom said.

I turned.

My mother was lying on top of her comforter. "Close the light."

"But I *did* hear someone."

"CLOSE THE LIGHT, Baby."

I groaned and did as I was told.

Back in my room, I found Go gnawing at the corner of the Creamsicle box. I yanked it from her jaws, then went to my window and raised the blinds. I held my breath. I could see the shed among the branches, the dark hollows of its windows, and that door—closed, like it'd never moved the whole night.

I listened.

Nothing.

Still, I didn't feel any better.

I dropped the blinds.

chapter 11

I woke up with an empty Creamsicle box in my clutches and to the sound of Go licking a wrapper on the floor. Sun filtered in through the blinds. As far as I knew, nothing unusual had happened the rest of the night. Or if it had, I'd been way too asleep to hear it.

By the time I walked into school, I was more than eager to see Tom. Somehow, just the thought of him calmed me. As I sat at my desk, I decided I'd leave him another note to tell him about the strange things that had been going on the last couple of days. *He'd* take me seriously.

I waited for the bus kids to arrive. Soon, Mayo and Dana came in, and we said our hellos as the rest of the class filtered in. "Paris," Mayo said, taking her seat, "I brought my birthday journal to take notes about you-know-what."

I turned to Mayo and smiled. "Can't wait to fill it up."

The bell rang.

I faced front as Mrs. Wembly shut the door to start class. That's when I noticed something was wrong—Tom's seat was empty.

"Class," Mrs. Wembly began, "I'm afraid I have some bad news. Tom hurt himself during basketball practice yesterday. He's got a broken arm and a mild concussion."

"He banged himself up good," Jay burst out. "Hit the basketball post on a fake. Maybe suffered some brain damage."

Mayo muttered under her breath, "*Please*, Tom already had brain damage."

I swallowed. Tom was hurt?

Mrs. Wembly sighed. "Let's not blow this out of proportion, Jay. Mrs. Cox assured me he'll be fine. Now, who wants to run his homework to him so he doesn't fall behind?"

Jay took the job, and Mrs. Wembly started the day's lesson as if Tom's accident was no big deal. But all I could think was, *a broken arm and a concussion?* I pictured Tom laid up in bed with gauze wrapped around his head and his arm in a sling. I might not see him for weeks! My stomach dropped.

I clutched my midsection. *What was that?*

Nervousness crept through my body, and suddenly, my heart began to pound in my chest. My palms got all sweaty. *Tom will be fine.* Mrs. Wembly said so. But I couldn't calm myself. In fact, the more I thought about him, the faster my heart beat and the sweatier my palms got.

Something was wrong with me.

I looked around. Everyone thought math was more interesting than whatever it was I had.

Take it easy, Paris. Maybe you're just worried Tom won't be able to help you with the Dare.

Yeah, that's it.

But as I glanced at Tom's desk again, my stomach

slipped another six notches. This was more than just worry.

Did I have a crush on Tom?!

"Paris Pan!"

The classroom came back into focus.

"Paris!" Mrs. Wembly snapped.

I blinked. "Um . . . yes?"

"Care to reduce this fraction for us?" My teacher held out her chalk. "Or are we too busy daydreaming this morning?"

I noticed Mayo giving me a strange look and I quickly got up. I hurried to the front.

The rest of the morning, between math problems and diagramming sentences, all I could think about was Tom. How we shared a moment in the woods when I lost Go . . . His first note to me with the cute little spelling mistake . . . Our close encounter at the fishing shack . . . The discreet looks we gave each other while Mayo yelled at him at lunch . . . Somewhere in there, the lunch bell rang, and we left the classroom.

"Paris!" Mayo said. "Are you hearing a word I'm saying?"

I looked around me. I was sitting on the steps, and I didn't even remember how I got there. "What?"

Mayo cocked her head. "Man, you are spacey today."

"Sorry," I said. "I was just thinking about our . . . our history quiz this afternoon."

"Well, forget history; we're on to science now."

"Science?"

"Our project," Dana said. "Mayo was saying we have to go to the library again. Day after tomorrow."

"Friday?" I said. "Why not today?" Not that that was what I wanted to do.

"Today is game day," Mayo replied. "And I have a dentist appointment on Thursday."

I groaned. "We have a game *today*?"

"Paris, we're playing Liberty Hill tonight," Dana said. "Remember? Six o'clock. The coach has only been pounding it into our heads all week!"

Mayo studied me. "You know what, Dana? She looks sort of funny. Her eyes are bloodshot."

"Maybe she's got something," Dana said.

I stared at her.

Bingo.

● ● ●

After school, I went straight home. I sat at my desk and fought this overwhelming urge to call Tom. I wanted to see how he was doing. I wanted to know he was okay. But calling him was out of the question. What if somebody found out?

Still, I felt like I had to do something. I'd make Tom a card. I wouldn't put my name on it, just like our notes. That would be safe. At the top of a piece of construction paper, I wrote, *GET WELL, TOM!* I drew a stick figure lying in bed with a bandaged head and a slinged arm. Next, I sketched a balloon above stick man's head and wrote, *At least I get to miss school!*

I heard my bedroom door bang open. I quickly shoved the card under a book. "What, Verona?"

"It's Athens, dummy."

I turned to look.

"Mom has to work late tonight. I told her I could take you guys to the game."

My mouth fell open. "You *volunteered*?"

"Be ready by five thirty sharp," Athens said, ignoring my question. "I don't have all day to wait for you dorks."

After Athens left, I pulled my card out and studied my bandaged stick man. Tonight's game made me wish I was the one who was concussed instead.

An hour later, I was in the back of the Buick, right on time. Verona climbed into the front seat and flipped open the visor mirror to check her makeup. I saw her game face, and I could tell she was still planning to bust onto the court like a half-dressed pop star. My plan was simpler, less flash: One, stop thinking about Tom and focus on the game. Two, stay away from the ball and leave the game with all body parts intact. Three, stop thinking about Tom already!

Athens got in, and soon we were on the road. As I watched the trees go by my window, I remembered what Dana had told me right after school. "The Liberty Hill Muskrats are big"—they were all eighth graders, which put Sugar Lake in a surefire losing position.

After my brother dropped us off, Verona and I went to the locker room. *Holy cow.* My sister wasn't the only Bumblebee posing as a tramp. So were the clones. Every single one of them had their bellies exposed and wore their shorts so short, they made the Laker Girls look like nuns.

We sat through a fruitless pep talk—booyah!—then waited to be called.

Outside, Mr. Wolcott shouted, "And for the home team, welcome Sugar Lake's very own Bumblebees!"

Shania Twain's "Man! I Feel Like a Woman!" boomed over the loudspeakers. We trotted out to the roar of the crowd. "Give it up for—" The microphone screeched. The music died off. Verona and the clones struck a pose. Immediately, they started to cheer.

"We're the Bumblebees, check out this!
We shoot, we score, we just can't miss!
Don't believe us? Just don't care?
Then pucker up and put one there!"

They all stuck their butts out.

Coach Dobson's whistle fell out of her mouth. From the stands, a red-faced Mr. Carlisle waved his arms at Mr. Wolcott in the announcer box.

I grinned when I thought about how many days my sister would spend in detention.

Mr. Wolcott spoke. "The Bumblebee spirit is . . . uh . . . well, they are on tonight, aren't they, folks?" The music blasted out of the speakers again, and Mr. Carlisle smiled.

"Let's hear it for Coach Dobson and the Bumblebees!"

The crowd roared.

Verona was a hit.

Unbelievable.

The game started. I spent the first half running aimlessly around the court, attempting to distract an opponent a foot taller than me while Verona enjoyed every bit of her newfound love for basketball. Dana was right. We were getting whupped. But my sister played the game like her every shimmy mattered. The crowd enjoyed themselves so much, I thought they might even be happy we were losing.

Near the end of the last period, everyone, maybe even Liberty Hill, rooted for us. The buzzer went off. Sugar Lake lost 77–8. But by the look on Verona's face, you'd think we'd just won the Final Four.

My sister gushed to her friends in the locker room, "That was awesome!"

"Last year," one of them said, "we didn't score at all. We were great, Verona!"

Verona's face turned serious. "You think we should come up with a halftime routine next time?"

I opened my locker, stared at the mirror, and pretended to throw up.

"We did score," Mayo said.

I frowned at my reflection. How was I going to survive the season watching Verona gyrate to Shania?

After we changed, I said good-bye to my friends outside and waited for my sister to finish talking to a group of greasy ninth-grade boys who had suddenly taken an interest in her—*sick!* I bided my time by observing a bunch of skaters leaning against the side of the building. The entire group stood in too-cool-for-everyone positions. And that's when I spotted Athens, slipping away from the pack. *No way.*

My brother, hanging with those losers?

A couple of minutes later, a car horn honked, and there was the Buick.

I called to my sister, but I kept my eye on our car. "Come on, Verona."

She finished up her flirting session and we got into the Buick.

As soon as I snapped my belt in, I stared at Athens. *"Ummm . . ."*

My guilty brother adjusted his sunglasses in the mirror even though it was pitch black outside. "What are you um'ing about?"

"I know why you were so excited to give us a ride tonight." I pointed at the window. "You've been hanging out with the Future Dropouts of America!"

Verona turned. "Paris, what are you talking about?"

"Athens was with those . . . vagrants."

Verona studied him. "You were?"

"Paris!" Athens growled. The car launched forward. "You better not say a word to Mom."

Guilty as charged. "Or what?"

"Or I'll tell everyone in school about your boyfriend."

I closed my mouth.

"Boyfriend?" Verona said. "Who'd want to go out with you, nerdo?"

"No one," I replied. "I mean, I don't have a boyfriend." Athens couldn't possibly know about Tom.

"Yes, you do," Athens said. "I saw him knocking on your window like Romeo."

"Tom is not my boyfriend." *Oh, brother.* Why'd I say his name? I am stupid, stupid, stupid.

"Tom?!" Verona shrieked. "Isn't he brain-damaged?"

"He is NOT brain-damaged," I said.

"Oh yes, he is. Everyone says so. Why do you think he talks like *th-th-th-that*?!"

Athens shook his head. "Man, Paris. You know how to pick 'em."

"He probably can't even spell his own name," Verona added.

This had to stop. "I'll have you know, Tom spells fine!"

Shoot. I did it again!

"Ooh," Verona cooed, "you writing love notes to each other?"

My siblings chorused, "Paris and Tom sitting in a tree. *K-i-s-s-i-n-g!*"

After another painful ten minutes, we finally got home, and I went right to my room. I retrieved the card and studied my handiwork.

Face it, Paris. You are in love with Tom.

I thunked my head against my desk a few times, then heard the doorbell ring.

"I'll get it!" I yelled as I shoved my card into the drawer. I headed for the foyer, wondering who would be at our door at eight in the evening. Maybe it was Tom. *Ugh.* I shook my head vigorously. *Stop thinking about him.* "I'm coming!"

When I got to the door, I peered through the peephole.

The entrance light only brightened about seven feet of our walk. No one was there.

My body tensed.

Quit it, Paris. Just open the door. Maybe it's a short kid selling cookies.

I inched the door open. At my feet was a basket wrapped in colored cellophane, filled with candy. It had to be from Johnny's Bait and Tackle. I reached for the basket, then got the feeling that I was being watched. I peered into the night. "Hello?"

No one answered back.

"Who's there, Paris?" Verona looked over my shoulder. "Dang, bring it in!"

I cast a wary glance at the dark and picked up the basket. I set it on the entrance table. While Verona ripped open the wrapping, I read the card. "'Welcome to the neighborhood. Please stop by anytime for a visit. The Laney family.'"

Verona snagged a Milky Way. "What do you know? Being neighbors with the Freak has benefits." She headed to her room.

I turned back to the door, and on a whim, I looked

through the peephole again. I jumped when I saw Robin in her coat, standing on the walk.

She was staring at my house. It looked like she was debating something.

I put my hand on the knob and willed myself to turn it. But then voices started talking in my head.

Voice #1: Don't open that door! She's the Freak, remember?
Voice #2: Why not? She dropped off a big basket of candy. You should say thank you.
Voice #1: Now is not the time to be making nice with someone Mayo and Dana hate.
Voice #2: Yeah . . . but . . .
Voice #1: But what? Think of what's at risk here.

I bit my lip and held on to the knob a moment longer, then let go.

But as Robin walked away, I wondered if I had done the right thing.

When Mom came home, she spotted the basket and acted like I'd stolen it. *"Baby,* where you get this?"

I was lying on the living room couch, flipping through TV channels. "Present from our neighbors," I mumbled. Everything I saw reminded me of Tom. *Tired of being single?* Tom. *Suffering from a stomachache?* Tom. I sighed and clicked off the TV.

"We owe everybody," Mom said as she took off her coat. "Now we owe neighbor, too."

That was one way of looking at it.

"This weekend," Mom said, "we make wontons and take them over. *Ay-yuh*, when I have time for this?"

"Take them over?" I straightened. "To their house?"

"Wontons don't have legs." Mom peeked into the basket. "And egg rolls, too. We go on Sunday."

Wait a second. "You mean, *all of us*?"

Mom looked up. "Who has choice? Everyone go when Daddy come home."

Oh, man.

Another packet of Pop Rocks later, I tried to forget about my impending visit to Robin's and put the final touches on Tom's card. I examined my masterpiece for any obvious hints of my true feelings. Nope. The card was simply a nice gesture. Inside, I wrote,

I hope the damage isn't permanent. Get well soon.

I put the card into a stamped envelope and copied Tom's address from the school directory. As I slipped it into a pile of Mom's outgoing mail, I heard a faint *eeeeeeeer* outside.

Go growled and hopped up to the windowsill.

Fortunately, I was prepared this time. I went to my bed and reached under my covers. I brandished Daddy's Ultralite 440 staple gun in case some sicko was out there. It wasn't loaded, but I figured if this was pointed at anyone, who would care? Then I gripped Daddy's rechargeable eighteen-volt DeWalt flashlight in my other hand.

The thing was almost as big as a prison guard's night-stick. Though I still didn't believe in ghosts, I figured it couldn't hurt to be ready. Really ready.

I went to my window and thrust my weapons in front of me.

I let out a breath. Nothing. I directed my gaze toward the shed.

The door was open.

chapter 12

Thursday was completely uneventful. Tom was out from school again, which made the whole day seem kind of pointless. The only thing worth noting was that I didn't hear a thing at night. Of course, wearing a pair of Verona's old earmuffs to bed probably had something to do with that.

On Friday, however, school was more torturous than usual. Since Valentine's Day fell on the weekend, Mrs. Wembly passed out candied hearts early. In my handful, I got *Call Me Later, Be My Hero,* and *U R A Tiger.* All I did was stare at Tom's empty desk. At lunch, all Mayo talked about was the Dare. And during basketball practice, Verona and "the Honeys"—as their group was now called—worked out halftime routines while the rest of us did layups. "You know it—we're hot! Now let's go make that shot! Bumblebees, Bumblebees. *Bzzzz-sting!"* My sister threw up pom-poms. Apparently, Principal Carlisle thought the Honeys should be properly equipped. I hated my sister.

After practice, while everyone else got excited about a three-day weekend, Mayo, Dana, and I were back at the library. We huddled around the microfiche station as headline after headline zipped by.

"Mayo, could you slow down?" I whispered. "You're giving me a headache."

Mayo kept moving the slide plate. "But we've got only ten minutes left."

Like I was in any hurry to find you-know-who.

"Stop," Dana said suddenly. "Go back."

Mayo looked at the screen. "What, what did you see?"

"Go back," Dana repeated. "There!"

A black-and-white image of a purse-lipped girl with pigtails stared back at me. *Conlon Girl Reported Missing.* I swallowed.

"Amen," Mayo said. "We've finally found it."

"She's so quiet-looking," Dana commented.

Mayo leaned in closer and scanned the article. "This one doesn't say much. A call for help. Nothing new. I bet it gets better."

Practically every issue after that had a Conlon headline. *Terrific.*

"We don't have time to read them all." Mayo started digging in her bag. "How much change do you have?"

"None." I didn't have to look to know how poor I was.

Dana and Mayo gathered up loose coins.

"Print these out," Mayo instructed as she shoved a pile of change on the table toward me. "I'll make sure Mrs. Reynolds doesn't wander over." She got up.

Dana took Mayo's seat and slid the plate to an article. I didn't bother to read it; I was sure Mayo would give me the highlights later. I dropped a dime in the slot, and the copy machine whirred.

"Paris?" Dana said.

"Yes?"

She positioned the plate to another article. "You know the other day when you said you had a feeling you knew where you-know-who died? Somewhere near where you sleep?"

I dropped a coin, surprised she even remembered that. "Yeah, what about it?" The machine spat out a copy.

"Did you really mean it?"

"Well . . . I've just heard stuff from my room, that's all."

"Stuff?"

"You know, giggling, tapping . . ."

"Are you serious? How do you sleep at night?"

Should I tell her about my sleeping aids? I decided against it. No sense in providing evidence of my insanity. "I do the best I can."

Dana turned her attention to the screen and stopped at another article.

We listened to the copy machine hum.

"So have you seen anything?" Dana didn't look at me this time.

I thought about the shed door opening and closing and that awful dream I'd had. But I thought I knew what she was really getting at. "Like a ghost?"

Dana nodded.

"Nope." But the worried expression on her face got me thinking. Was I not the only one who was spooked by this? "Dana," I said quietly, "are you scared?"

"Of course not," she whispered.

"You are, aren't you?"

Dana hesitated, taking her hand off the slide plate. "Well, a little. But you can't tell Mayo I said that."

Now Dana seemed even more scared, like making Mayo upset would be worse than dying in the woods.

But me? I was overjoyed. "So am I, Dana. This is great! We can both tell Mayo that we don't want to do the Dare."

"No, we can't."

"Why not? We outnumber her. We can convince her it's a bad idea."

Dana glanced nervously at the stacks again. "Forget I said anything, okay?"

"But why?"

"If there's one thing I've learned about Mayo, it's that you don't get her mad," Dana said quietly.

"But she'll listen to us if we both talk to her," I whispered.

"No, what she'll do is treat us both like she does Robin."

"Oh, come on. She wouldn't do that."

"Yes, she would. You don't know what she did to Shelly Decker."

"What do you mean?"

"Fourth grade. We all used to be friends until Shelly decided she didn't want to do everything Mayo said. It was awful, Paris. Not a day went by that Mayo didn't try pulling the kind of stuff she does on Robin."

"So what happened to her?"

"Shelly's father got a new job and they moved. I bet she was thrilled to leave Sugar Lake. So if you tell Mayo, I'll just say you're the one who's scared."

I sat back in my chair. "You wouldn't."

"Who do you think Mayo would believe? You or me? I've known her since kindergarten."

This was a side to Dana I didn't know. "All right, fine. I won't breathe a word."

"Good." Dana put her hands back on the slide plate.

An awkward silence followed as I realized this business of friendship was getting more twisted by the minute.

Finally, Dana spoke up. "Look, don't get the wrong idea about Mayo. She can be a great friend, you know?"

"Yeah, I know." But I wasn't sure I believed it.

"All I want is for the three of us to get along, Paris. We'll get you-know-what over with and move on like normal people. That's what you want, too, right?"

I stayed quiet, flipping a coin in my hand as I thought over Dana's words.

"Paris, that is what you want, isn't it?"

"Yeah," I said with a sigh.

When Mayo returned, she rifled through the photocopies. "What do we have?"

"Well, we used most of the change," Dana replied.

"Do we have anything on where you-know-who was found?"

Dana and I looked at each other and shrugged.

Mayo glanced at the last copy and shook her head.

"They haven't found her in this one. I guess Dana and I will have to come again tomorrow." She turned to me. "When do you get back from your trip?"

"Trip?" Then I remembered what I'd told Mayo and Dana earlier. "Let's see . . . We're driving to . . . uh . . . St. Louis, so I'll be back Monday evening. Around seven." I figured the more specific I got, the more convincing my lie would sound.

Dana sighed. "It's too bad you're not going to be with us."

I held back a smile as we packed our things. "Yeah," I said. "What a shame."

● ● ●

That evening, while I was supposedly on my way to St. Louis, Mom and I were sitting at the dining table making appetizers for the Laneys. Mom had already planned most of the weekend out. Tonight, wontons. Tomorrow, clean the house. Then Sunday, forget Valentine's Day. The Pan family would be off to the Laneys'. And as for Monday, Mom hadn't gotten that far, but knowing her, we'd spend the day drywalling the garage. A whole extended weekend of fun-fun-fun.

"Baby, too much meat," Mom said, referring to my dumpling. She pointed at her wonton as an example, folded it into a neat little package, and set it on a tray next to the others.

I stared at the wrapper in my hand; a giant meatball

sat atop it. It looked fine to me. "Mom," I said, "do we really have to go to the Laneys'?"

Mom raised an eyebrow.

"I mean, can't we do like they did?" I said. "Let's just drop these puppies off on their doorstep."

"Why you don't want to go?" Mom said. "Something wrong with neighbors?"

"Well . . ." I wished I could tell her why making nice with Robin and her family could potentially scar me for life in the friendship department. But somehow, I knew Mom wouldn't get it.

The phone rang.

Mom wiped her hands and answered it.

I tried to seal up my dumpling, but the wrapper tore. Maybe Mom was right. My wonton was so big it could wear pants.

Mom covered the receiver with her hand. "Take Go out."

Go was sleeping by the patio door. "But she doesn't need to go out." I reached for another wrapper. Besides, it was Athens's job until midnight tonight. He wasn't getting by with a minute less.

"Baby!"

"Okay, okay." Jeez. I wiped my hands and scooted back from the table.

As I stepped outside with Go, the sun had already gone down, but I could still make out part of the yard from our house lights. I glanced at the dark shapes of the shed and the trees and stayed by the house. This time, I watched exactly where Go was going.

"One Mississippi . . . two Mississippi . . ."

Thankfully, Go trailed her nose along the side where I could see her. She was just a furry outline, but that was good enough. "Three Mississippi . . . four Mississippi . . ." She was below my window. I heard her sniffing at the ground, then the sound of her claws digging like crazy.

"Go, quit it!" Mom was not going to like a new pothole right by the house.

I tried to pull Go in, but she was pulling against the leash with the power of her hind legs. I was afraid her collar would pop off again. "Go, stop that!"

Fine. I'd have to get her. I heard her digging again, and when I got closer, dirt was flying.

"No!" I picked Go up and glanced at the hole she'd started. Great. It was big enough for Mom to notice. Then in the moonlight, I saw something shine from the base of the hole. It was dark and curved, about the size of my fingertip, half buried. I froze.

Is that an eye?

I swallowed.

Don't be ridiculous.

"Baby!"

I looked over my shoulder. I could make out my mother standing by the door. "What?"

"Come in," she ordered. *"Now."*

I glanced back at the hole again and shoved the dirt back into place with my shoe.

I scooped up my dog, then my breath caught in my

throat. Mayo and Dana's voices were ringing in my head. "Shiny, porcelain faces, gazing skyward."

Was that a doll?

I shook my head.

No. It was just a . . . a marble. That's it.

I rushed back to the house anyway. When I got inside, my mother was in the kitchen, trying to stuff a whole tray of wontons and a bowl of meat into the freezer.

No Ziploc? Something was wrong. "Mom?"

She turned, worry written all over her face. "Get my purse. We go Oklahoma City."

I stared at her. *Huh?*

Mom called for my siblings.

"Daddy's had a heart attack."

● ● ●

We took both cars. Mom was staying overnight. Verona rode with my brother, and I rode with Mom. She gripped the steering wheel so hard her hands were practically white. A million questions zipped through my mind.

"Daddy is going to be okay, right, Mom?"

She didn't respond.

"What did the doctors say?"

No answer. It was like she wasn't even there.

"Mom, please, say something!"

She blinked. "Baby, this not good time."

Not good time? My jaw tightened. I wanted to ask if

there ever was a good time. It wasn't like I was inquiring about the weather. But I knew better than to start something now.

I stared out the window and told myself Daddy was fine. *Just fine.*

An hour and a half later, we pulled up to a hospital that was a throwback to the 1960s. I gaped at the peeling paint and the olive green doors. *Just fine,* my foot.

But the scariest thing about the place was my very own father.

I saw the oxygen mask over Daddy's face and all the tubes. He was so pale. Verona rushed in and threw herself across him. "DADDY!" I just stood there, numb with fear.

"Hi, Doro-see," Daddy said. "Come, son. Come, Baby. Good you see me for a change." Athens and I stood on one side of the bed, while Mom stood next to Verona. My father patted my hand. I cringed when I saw the IV poking from his wrist.

"I'm fine, children," Daddy said. "I'm powerful like De-Walt." He chuckled at his own joke.

Verona sobbed harder. Athens and I told her to shut up.

A doctor stepped in. "Mrs. Pan? May I speak with you?"

Mom left the room, and Daddy told us what had happened. "I get strange feeling." He put a hand on his chest. "I think, chili dog for lunch. Shouldn't buy something from street. Mom right. I fall, then Hank catch me and rush me here . . ."

As my dad went on, all I could do was stare at his IV. I wondered if it hurt, if the heart attack hurt . . .

Athens whopped the back of my head. "PARIS. Dad's talking to you."

"Huh?" I blinked. "What?"

Daddy took off his mask. "How's basketball? Mom tell me you girls play good."

Ha! And how would she know? I almost laughed, but then it didn't seem like the right moment for it. "Yup," I managed.

"Good, good. I know I raise good daughters. Your mother teach you right."

Daddy moved on to Athens. He asked if he'd gotten a start on his college applications just as Mom stepped in. "You did it, Daddy—three days in hospital. Two months, no work."

Two months?

My father pumped his fist in the air, whipping his tubes with it. "Yes!"

I knew Daddy's reaction was an attempt to show everyone how great the situation was, but I wasn't fooling myself. The coming weeks, Mom would probably live at the office trying to earn the income of two people. And my father? He'd ponder our uncertain future over Hershey's bars and beef snacks on the Pan family couch.

When we got home, I was so tired, I could hardly pay attention to the fact that Athens dropped us off and didn't come in. Mom was going to go directly to work tomorrow from the hospital so she could put in some Saturday overtime.

I dragged myself to bed, popped on my earmuffs, and studied the ceiling. I thought about Daddy. Him trying to look strong. Saying he was powerful like DeWalt. I pushed back the blankets and grabbed *Health and Wellness* from my bookshelf. Then I caught a glimpse of my window and remembered the "marble" I'd seen just outside it. Suddenly, I had no desire to spend another night in my room with the house so empty. I took off my earmuffs and curled up on Daddy's favorite spot on the living room sofa. I turned to a section titled "Caring for Your Heart" and started reading.

● ● ●

I must have fallen asleep because the next thing I knew, it was the middle of the night. Go was whining, and I realized I was still in the living room. My *Health and Wellness* book was in my lap.

Go pawed at the patio door. My deal with Athens was over, so I had to let Go out. I shuffled over to Go, hooked her up, and opened the door. Under the glow of the house lights, she sniffed around as I leaned against the doorway. My bare feet froze. I struggled to keep my eyes open.

Go's yip made me jump. Had I been asleep? She stared at me, a doll at her feet.

Every part of my body flipped on. *A doll. The hole by*

my window. I leapt back and yanked the door shut. Go studied me, then wrestled with the doll's arm. I opened my mouth to scream for help, but stopped myself.

I dropped Go's leash on the floor and hurried to the kitchen. I picked up the phone to dial 9-1-1, then paused.

What was I going to say?

My dog found a doll in my yard. No . . .

A killer left a doll in my yard. No . . .

I have a doll that belongs to a dead girl? No . . .

I looked over at the patio door.

Wait. Where was Go?

I put down the phone and crept toward the sliding door. All I could see was her leash disappearing into the trees. This was not good. Before I could make up my mind about what to do next, Go trotted into view. I let out a breath. She padded across the patio and yipped at the glass.

Wait a second. Where was the doll?

Had I imagined the whole thing?

I blinked.

Go was standing there, waiting to come in.

I had to know if the doll was real, but I wasn't going out there to look for it. I glanced at Go's muddy paws. If Go had dug it up, there'd be evidence by my window. I quickly let her in and wiped her feet. We went to my room. I turned on my lights and yanked up the blinds.

Once my eyes adjusted, I could see the woods and the shed. The door was closed. A gust of wind shook the trees. My stomach tightened as I opened my window and peeked over the ledge. Light from my room spilled onto the ground.

When I saw the spot where Go had been digging yesterday, I couldn't breathe.

All the dirt was in place like I'd left it. I even saw my shoe prints on the surface.

I jerked my head in, shut the window, then dropped the blinds. Had I made up both the marble *and* the doll? Was I seeing things?

I fumbled through my bookshelves and pulled out my *Psychology Today* book. This time, I was trying to figure out what was wrong with *me*. I skimmed the pages for anything that might apply. *Obsessive compulsive disorder. Phobias.* So far, nothing about visions. Until I came to chapter five. *Psychosis.* I swallowed.

Some people suffer from a mental impairment that is marked by disturbances of sensory perception (hallucinations). As a result, they may be unable to separate the real from the unreal.

I thought about that scary dream I'd had—or was it a dream?

The tapping and the giggling—or had I made that up?

The doll—was that an illusion created by my *impaired* mind?

I read on.

Maybe I was one of two million Americans who suffer from the illness in a given year.

Maybe I was an atypical case where episodes could begin during adolescence.

Maybe I was . . .

The bolded words leapt from the page.

A paranoid schizophrenic.

I closed the book, feeling slightly comforted. It was a possibility.

Mental illness in the Pan family? Why not?

If I'm seriously ill, all I have to do is pretend none of this is happening. But even as I glanced at my window again, I wondered if a killer or a ghost was having a great time toying with my mind.

I had to plan for the worst-case scenario.

I scooted every piece of furniture I could move against the window. When I got into bed, I had my staple gun at the ready and the flashlight in my hands. I lay on my side, then pointed my flashlight toward the window and turned it on.

chapter 13

When morning came, I was lying in bed, hugging Daddy's DeWalt, staring at the tower I'd created with my desk chair, the wastebasket, and a short bookshelf. I realized I needed to talk to someone.

I needed Tom.

It had been three days, fifteen hours, and twenty-nine minutes since I had last seen him, roughly.

At this point, he was the only person who could make me feel sane again. I thought about how I should reach him. I couldn't use Robin's tree—no telling when he'd be back at school to pick up the note. There was just one option.

I shrank under the covers.

I had to call him.

That evening, I waited for the one time the phone was certain to be clear—while Verona was in the shower. But she was blabbing on the phone, taking her time. I waited, the handset from the kitchen in my grip and the school directory in my lap.

An hour later, Verona hung up at last. Her footsteps headed toward the bathroom. The toilet flushed, and the shower turned on. I had thirty minutes, maybe forty. My fingers flew across the buttons.

A woman answered. "Hello?"

Shoot. I had hoped Tom would pick up. "Hi . . . uh . . . is Tom there?"

"Yes, who's calling?"

"It's Paris."

"Paris?" the lady said. "Are you a friend from school?"

"Uh . . . we're in the same class."

"Really? What's your last name?"

"It's Pan," I said. "I just moved here."

"Oh, of course," the lady said. "The *Pans.* Mrs. Laney said you moved into the Con—" She stopped herself. "I mean, the new house your father built. Isn't that right?"

"Yes, ma'am." I let out a breath. *Please get Tom already?*

The next five minutes, Tom's mother kept yakking, telling me about how she wanted to invite the entire Pan family over for dinner—"We're practically neighbors!"— then she went into a long-winded explanation of how she hadn't gotten around to asking since she's been so busy.

I rubbed the back of my neck. Now I knew why Tom could barely talk. His mother had used up all the words.

Go cocked her head at me.

"Well, Paris, now that Tom's better, ask your parents which day works best for a get-together."

I heard the shower turn off. *Wait a second*—Verona was done already? My grip on the phone tightened. "I don't think we can make it."

"But why not, Paris? Is your mother home? Maybe if I speak to her directly . . ."

"I really don't think we can," I repeated. *Get Tom, woman!* Verona's footsteps headed past my room.

"Are you sure? What about the following week?"

Jeez, lady! "My dad's had a heart attack, okay?!"

I closed my mouth. I couldn't believe I'd just said that. The line went silent.

"Oh, dear," Mrs. Cox finally said. "I had no idea . . ."

The back of my eyes started to hurt; Go looked at me funny.

I heard the phone change hands. "G-G-Give it to me, Mom!

"H-H-Hello?"

It was Tom. Hearing his voice made something get stuck in my throat. I tried to swallow.

"Paris," Tom said, "we need to t-t-talk." His voice was serious. "I g-g-got your c-c-card."

My lip trembled.

"P-P-Paris?"

"PARIS!" my sister barked over the phone. "Is that Brain-Damaged Boy?!"

My door flung open. Verona had a towel on her head and her phone to her ear.

I hung up.

"I'm expecting an important call from Jane at eight thirty sharp!"

I choked back tears.

The phone rang.

"Verona Pan speaking . . . Oh, hey, Jane!"

My sister gave me a dirty look and slammed my door.

I waited a few seconds, then let the tears run.

I cried about everything—the Dare, the doll, but most of all, I cried about Daddy.

• • •

It was almost midnight when I woke up on the floor. Go was sitting next to me, scratching her ear with her hind leg. I stared at the hard tissue balled in my hand, and my body relaxed. Daddy was okay. I headed out of my room to wash my face and spotted the school directory next to my bed—the call.

Verona called Tom brain-damaged, and I hung up on him.

Terrific. He might never speak to me again. I had to fix this. I opened my door and stepped into the hall. Mom's sudden shouts from the living room stopped me. "Where you go?!"

I could make out Verona in her pajamas hovering at the end of the hall, listening.

"None of your business!" Athens said.

I tiptoed over to my sister. "What's going on?" I whispered.

Verona scowled. "Mom caught Athens sneaking in."

Sneaking in? Those friends of his were a bad influence. BAD!

"I said, *where you go?*" Mom's voice was ice.

"Nowhere," Athens said. "Worry about Dad, not me. He's the one who had a heart attack!"

I gulped. Was my brother trying to get killed?

"Your daddy work for everything," Mom cried. "You so ungrateful—never appreciate what he do for us!"

"All you and Dad did was practically guarantee I'd have no life, and now I'm finally trying to have one, so just *stay out of it*." Athens headed toward us.

Verona whispered, "Let's go!"

"Wait!" Mom ordered.

My sister and I stopped.

"You grounded! No car."

I heard keys hit the coffee table.

Athens was coming.

Verona and I scrambled so fast, we tripped on each other and fell to the carpet.

My brother stopped in front of us. *"What the?"* He switched on the lights. "I hope you were taking notes because this is what you get to look forward to!" He stepped over us, went down the hall, and slammed his door.

● ● ●

The next morning, I tried to stay in my room, afraid that if I ventured out and even glanced at Mom the wrong way, she'd have a breakdown. But I had to leave eventually; I didn't know how long a twelve-year-old could go without food or water, but by ten forty-five I'd have sworn

I was dying. I crept down the hall to the kitchen, opened the fridge, and went for the OJ.

"Baby?"

Mom's voice jolted me and I almost dropped the carton. My mother was standing in her bathrobe at the other end of the kitchen. "Yeah, Mom?" She looked more tired than her regular tired. I tried not to stare.

She took down a mug from a cupboard. "Today you and sister help me get house ready for Daddy." She grabbed the coffeepot. "Then tomorrow we finish making wontons for Laneys. You take it to them before Daddy comes home. I won't go with you." She turned on the water.

"But—"

Mom froze by the sink and glared at me. "But what?"

"What about Verona?"

She shut off the water. "I see," Mom began. "Everyone has their own life, right?" Her voice quivered. "No one cares what I think . . ."

Here we go . . .

". . . Everyone does what they do. Who ask me?"

I hated it when she did this. It wasn't my fault our family was screwed up. "Okay, okay. I'll do it."

"After that, you practice violin."

I frowned. *"Violin?"*

She tilted her head. "You and sister practice every day, right?"

I thought about the untouched case under my bed. "Uh-huh."

"Good. When Daddy come home, you all play for him. Now we clean." Mom called for my sister. "Wa-wa!"

Hey. "What about Athens?"

"He work on college application."

"That's not fair!"

My mother gave me a look.

"Never mind."

Over the next few hours, we scrubbed, swept, and dusted to make our house seem newer than before. It was amazing what hard labor could do for my mood. I decided going to Robin's tomorrow wasn't so bad. All I'd have to do was zip over, dump the appetizers at their door, and *run.* I even thought Tom would understand why I hung up on him yesterday. I mean, what was I supposed to do with Verona on the phone? Let her call him names? It was a defensive move on my part, and Tom probably knew it. Besides, it was Valentine's Day. Surely, he could find it in his heart to forgive me. I trailed the cloth along the edge of the dining table. *He is Tom, after all.*

My stomach flip-flopped.

Stop it, Paris.

A couple of hours later, we finished cleaning. Then, Mom made us rearrange furniture and put out candles and decorator pillows I didn't even know we owned. She kept saying Daddy would like it better this way, no, that way, no, try like this. When I helped Mom hang artwork above the fireplace, requiring a full-sized nail and a matching hole to fit, I almost fainted.

Afterward, I went back to my room exhausted. I lay on my bed and stared at the ceiling, wondering what Mayo and Dana were doing. Watching movies, making brownies. Surely their day had been more fun than mine.

Mom came in. She chucked a red envelope onto my bed. "This in mailbox." She raised an eyebrow. "Better not be from boy. You too young!" She shut the door.

I picked up the card-sized envelope resting on my comforter. Was I getting a card . . . on Valentine's Day? *No way.*

There was no return address or stamp. But there was my name. Centered across the front in block letters.

Could it be?

Was it from . . . Tom?

I clutched the envelope, my fingers shaking. Maybe he thought *my* card and phone call were special. Maybe he thought *I* was special. I had to open this somewhere private. I dashed into the bathroom and locked the door.

I sat on the edge of the tub and studied the envelope again, relishing every detail before I opened it. I admired how lovely my name looked, written in what could only be Tom's broken-arm penmanship. I took in the vibrant hue of the envelope. How did he know red was my favorite color?

Maybe . . . I carefully opened the envelope . . . he had a crush on me, too.

I slipped the card out. The front was simple. Just the beautifully scripted words . . . *Happy Valentine's Day.* This would make such a fabulous addition to my album, and I knew I would cherish the words inside for the rest of my life.

My stomach fluttered. I opened the card.

I just want to be your friend.

There it was—the letters blurred in front of me—the all-time worst rejection a girl could ever get.

I sat there wondering how this could have happened. I tried to remember the last words he shared with me on the phone. He said we needed to talk. That he'd gotten my card. *Oh, brother.* I leaned my head against the shower tile. *Take a hint, Paris.* Making a card for him, calling him, then hanging up on him was probably a bit much. *What were you thinking?*

Back in my room, I opened my desk drawer and tossed the card in. I held back something welling up in my throat. *It's okay, Paris. Getting dissed by the least desirable boy in seventh grade, next to Jay, isn't easy. But think of it this way. You're a new woman. You're free.*

I shut the drawer.

Go started whining. I turned to look at her. She stared at my door.

I groaned and went straight to Athens's room. I couldn't take it anymore.

Go followed.

I knocked.

No one answered. *That's weird.* Wasn't Athens grounded?

I tried one more time, and just as I was about to tell Mom that her son was probably climbing out the window, I heard my brother grumble, "What?"

I opened the door. Athens was sitting at his desk, rifling through a bunch of college applications.

"Go has to go," I said.

"So? Our deal is over, remember? Six days and that was it."

"I thought we'd make a new one."

"Why?"

"Because ... I've ... I've got scoop ..." I hoped I'd picked the right subject. "On Roxy."

He frowned. "And?"

"Well, don't you care?"

He turned back to his applications and started filling one out. "No, not really."

This wasn't good. "So you know everything about her ... and Ty?"

"Ty? *Again?*" Athens looked at me. "What do you know?"

Relief washed over me. "No way. Deal first. One month."

"One month? Forget it." He pointed to the door. "Get out."

"Three weeks, then. I promise it's *good*. This is a bargain."

"Two weeks and that's it."

"Deal." I had only hoped for a week anyway.

I told him everything. Everything I could make up. About how Mayo had seen Roxy and Ty hooking up in Mr.

Seaver's truck. How Mayo said Ty liked to meet Roxy behind the Dumpster at the high school. All their secret trysts in sordid places. "... And you don't even want to know what they're doing for Valentine's Day."

When I finished, Athens couldn't even look me in the eye. "Thanks," he mumbled. He picked up Go and pushed past me.

No, thank you.

That night, I crawled into bed and performed what was quickly becoming a nightly ritual. I arranged my pillow, the sheets, the flashlight, and the staple gun. Just as I was about to pop on the earmuffs, Go started growling from the foot of my bed. *What now?*

All I could hear was Verona chatting it up with some cheesy music in the background. Go approached the window. Then I heard it, too.

Voices.

A girl. Upset. Arguing. Someone talking back. A boy maybe. Or a man . . .

Eeeeeeeeeeeer.

I snapped on the earmuffs and closed my eyes.

This is just your mind, Paris.

But I couldn't stop the sounds from echoing in my head.

I opened my eyes and looked at Go. She was still at the window.

Maybe Go was sick, too.

chapter 14

Presidents' Day is usually a holiday when I sleep in and lounge in front of the TV, but this year? No way. While Mom and Verona worked on making a welcome home meal for Daddy, I was hurrying down our wooded slope, carrying two trays of wontons and egg rolls. Most parents who loved their children wouldn't let their daughters make the quarter-mile walk in the winter, but Mom said, "Why you worry? Sun still out." By the time I climbed the steps to the Laneys' porch, my teeth were chattering and my hands were practically frozen to the trays.

I stood in front of the door. The shades were drawn and a sign hanging in a window read *Closed.* I wondered if the Laneys had a different entrance for personal use. *Oh, who cares? I'll just leave these right here and make a break for it.* But before I could do just that, Fritz started barking his head off inside. "Who's there?" I heard Mrs. Laney say. *Shoot.* The door jingled open. "Paris?"

Mrs. Laney was standing in front of me, Fritz in her arms.

"Paris, you've got to be cold," she said. "Come in." She ushered me inside, set down the dog, and took my neighborly offering from me.

I started to protest, but I shut up when the warmth of

Mrs. Laney's shop enveloped me and the smell of baking cookies hit my nose. Fritz put his paws on my legs, his tail whipping back and forth. Maybe I could stay for a minute. I glanced at the darkened windows—who would know?

Mrs. Laney placed the trays on the counter and took my coat. "How about some hot chocolate? Then you can tell me all about what you brought."

I smiled. "Um . . . sure."

Mrs. Laney disappeared behind the curtain, and I kneeled to ruffle Fritz's fur. I wondered where Robin was.

The next thing I heard was whispering and scuffling, then Robin burst through the curtain, like someone had pushed her through.

We looked at each other, and a thick blanket of unease settled over the room.

"Hi," I managed to say. A part of me felt like I owed it to Robin to at least be polite after what I'd seen Mayo do to her.

Robin's gaze fell to her shoes. "Hi." Her voice was almost a whisper. Fritz padded over to her, and Robin picked him up.

What now? I racked my brain for something to say. "Fritz is cute."

Robin held him close. "Thanks."

"So . . . uh . . . I've got a dog, too. Her name is Go. She's not the brightest, but she can sit, stay, shake hands . . ." Clearly, I was just trying to fill up the air with words. What was taking Mrs. Laney so long? "I tried to teach her to play dead once, but she's not so great at holding still. What about Fritz? Does he know any tricks?"

Good thinking, Paris. Throw the ball in her court.

Robin hesitated for a second. Then she nodded and set Fritz down. She turned her palm to the ceiling and raised her forearm. "Stand."

Fritz stood up.

Robin rotated her wrist. "Turn."

Fritz hopped on his feet and did a 360.

"Wow," I said. "What else does he know?"

Robin looked at me, then grabbed a phone book off the counter. She set it on the floor and opened it to the middle. Fritz's tail thumped the floor.

"Read," Robin said.

Fritz stared at the book, took his paw, and dragged it over a page. He slid the page until it flipped to the other side. He did it again. It really looked like he was reading. *Get out.* "Does he order pizza, too?"

Robin smiled just as Mrs. Laney stepped in with a platter of cookies and a couple of steaming mugs.

"Well, now," Mrs. Laney said, "it seems like you girls are enjoying yourselves."

I swallowed. I'd just realized what I'd been doing— getting chummy with the person everyone thought was a freak. I didn't say anything. Robin didn't either. She put the phone book away and grabbed her dog.

Fortunately, Robin's mom was too busy setting up the perfect atmosphere for Robin and me to become BFFs to notice anything had changed between us. "I've got M&M

cookies." She put the platter on the counter. "And I made the hot cocoa with real Hershey's."

I knew that if I didn't do something now, I'd never be able to leave. "Actually, Mrs. Laney, I don't mean to be rude, but I just remembered my mom needs me home. I'm supposed to help her with something. Can I take a rain check?"

I felt bad, but it couldn't be helped. I gave Robin a look that meant, *I'm sorry, but you understand, right?* I'm not sure it translated.

"Well . . . I . . . uh . . ." Mrs. Laney fiddled with her hair. "Are you sure you need to go?"

I nodded.

"Then at least take some cookies with you." She grabbed a plastic bag from under the counter and dropped a couple into the sack. "Please come and see us anytime, all right? I mean it." She held out the bag.

"Sure," I said, taking the cookies from her. I pulled my coat off the rack. "Thanks for everything, Mrs. Laney." I put the coat on and slipped the bag in my pocket. I glanced at Robin. "Bye."

I reached for the door.

"Paris?" Mrs. Laney said. "Thank your mother for the . . . uh . . ." She stared at the trays.

"Egg rolls and wontons," I said. "Just fry them up when you're ready to eat them."

I opened the door, then shut it behind me without looking back.

As I headed home, I felt guilty for leaving so quickly.

Maybe I was no better than Mayo. I glanced at the trees and fast-walked up the slope. *No, don't say that. And even if it were true, Mayo's not such a bad person, remember? If it weren't for her, you'd be spending your lunches like Robin. You'd be suffering through school and basketball alone.*

You owe Mayo for taking you in. You're doing the right thing.

I shoved my hands deeper into my pockets and felt the bag of cookies under my fingers. They were still warm.

Suddenly, I heard a twig crack, and I ran the rest of the way.

● ● ●

That evening, as I waited for Daddy to come home, I sat on the floor in my room. Go was sitting in front of a phone book. I pointed to it. "Read."

She sneezed and lay down.

"Oh, come on." I'd been working on this trick for nearly thirty minutes.

I heard the phone ring. Probably one of Verona's dumb friends.

Moments later, Verona was at my door. "It's for you again. Breaking records, aren't we?" She snickered and dropped the phone onto my bed. I did an impression of my sister's ugly face, then got up and shut the door. Before I picked up the handset, I was struck with this hope that it might be Tom.

Wait a second. If it were Tom, Verona would have paraded around the house with the phone, shouting, "Paris, it's your lover boy!"

I frowned. "Hello?"

"Hey, Paris," Mayo said. "Glad you're back. I don't want to say too much over the phone, but I had to tell you the news. We got some good stuff for our science project. Isn't that great?"

I faked enthusiasm. "Terrific!"

"Can you go to Dana's house tomorrow? Probably better if we don't talk about this at school, either. I was thinking we could meet up before the game."

"Actually . . ." Maybe I should tell Mayo about what happened to Daddy. Perhaps she'd give me a get-out-of-the-Dare-free card while I nursed my father back to health. Ha! *I dream.* "Tomorrow sounds fine."

After we hung up, I tossed the phone into the hall— "I'm done!"—closed the door, and leaned against it. Then I glanced at my bookshelf and stared at my photo album.

This better be worth it.

I heard the garage door. *Daddy. Finally.*

"Baby! Wa-wa! Athens!" my father called. "I'm home."

"Daddy!" I said, as I ran out of my room.

"Wowowow!" He stood in the foyer. "House looks great!" Mom was standing next to him. She dropped her keys in her purse and helped him with his coat.

I ran up to my father and gave him a hug. Verona wasn't too far behind. "Hey, Daddy."

He looked fifty times better than he did at the hospital. He was normal-Daddy color and everything. "How are you feeling?" I asked.

He flexed his arm. "No heart attack stop me!"

He put one arm around Verona and one around me. Then he took in a deep breath. "Mmmm-mmm-mmm. When we eat? I tired of hospital."

Mom hung up her coat. "Soon. Everything almost done." She headed for the kitchen.

"Hey." Athens stepped into the foyer.

"Son," Daddy said, "how you doin'?"

"All right," my brother replied, but he didn't sound very convincing.

"Something wrong?" Daddy let go of me. "Or just college applications?"

"Yeah, something like that."

Daddy patted him on the back. "Good, good. Well, tonight, children, Mom say we have best dinner ever. Now where violins?"

While Mom set the table, Daddy and Athens sat on the living room couch while Verona and I stood in front of them with our instruments in the ready position. We played a minuet, but we might as well have been performing something Go had made up. My sister's bow went up. Mine went down. She played a note. I hit one kind of like it. I could just see Mozart looking down at us from above and slapping his forehead.

"Beautiful," Daddy commented.

Athens and Go groaned.

"Chi fan le!" Mom yelled from the kitchen. Time for dinner.

We filed into the dining room, and I checked out the spread. It was like Thanksgiving reborn on the table— thick, buttery mashed potatoes, roasted corn covered in salt, candied yams with marshmallows, turkey *and* ham?! . . . I glanced at Daddy and my excitement faded. I thought about what my *Health and Wellness* book had said about a heart-friendly diet. I elbowed my mother as she set down a bowl of stuffing. "Daddy can't have all of this stuff."

"One night okay."

Who was going to tell *him* that? My father tucked a napkin into his collar and sniffed a bowl of mashed potatoes. I made a mental note to watch his portions. Seconds would be out of the question.

After everyone was seated, Daddy said, "How about we pray this time, huh? Today we have lots to thank for."

We bowed our heads.

"Dear Lord," he began, "you give us three lovely children, keep food on our table . . ."

Daddy could go on for hours, talking to God. I peeked at the turkey and was reminded how long it'd been since I'd had a real meal. I looked at my fork and determined how fast I could grab the utensil, spear the leg, and get it back onto my plate. I had a two-second lead on my brother, based on our respective distances from the bird. The drumstick was mine.

Daddy took a breath. ". . . You give me second life . . .

Thank you, Lord, for your letting us see what need to be done."

"Amen." *Let's eat.* I stabbed the drumstick with my fork.

"We're not moving anymore," Daddy announced. He beamed from the end of the table and squeezed Mom's hand.

Forks clanged to platters. I held my turkey leg in the air. "What?"

"What Daddy say is," Mom explained, "go here, go there—no good for you children."

"You mean, we're staying—" I said.

"Forever?" Verona finished.

My parents nodded.

"Yes!" my sister squealed. "The Honeys will live on!"

I dropped my drumstick and looked around me. *No way.* How was I going to survive the rest of my life *here*?

Athens stabbed the turkey on his plate like he wanted it dead twice.

"What's wrong?" Daddy said. "Athens, Baby, we thought you be happy."

Happy? I needed a decent education, to live past twelve, to sleep without earmuffs, a flashlight, and a power tool.

"Unbelievable." Athens tossed his napkin onto the table. "You waited my entire life to decide this?!" He pushed back and left the room.

I stared at Athens's full plate. He was *mad.*

"Athens!" my mother called.

Daddy touched Mom's arm. "Let him go. He be okay. Baby? What you think? This is good, right?"

I was still staring at my brother's plate. Then I looked at my parents.

I picked up my napkin and scooted back.

My mother stared me down.

I tossed my napkin like my brother had and went straight to my room.

● ● ●

In my bedroom, I kneeled over a newspaper spread across the floor. I put the final touches on something I should have made a long time ago.

My Last Will and Testament
by Paris Pan
Hereby witnessed on this date by Go Pan.

I lifted my dog's inked paw and pressed it onto the paper.

My door opened. Daddy poked his head in. "Baby?"

I stuffed the will under the bed. "What?"

Go padded up to my father. Daddy surveyed the blue paw prints on the newspaper. "What you doing?"

I shrugged and reached for the Kleenex on my nightstand. "Nothing." I called my dog over and wiped her foot.

"You want to talk?" Daddy said.

"About what?"

He closed the door. "Why you don't want to stay?"

I didn't say anything.

"Baby?" Daddy pressed. "Is it the shed?"

I glanced at the window and nodded. But that didn't begin to cover it. "It's still there, Daddy."

My father sat on my bed. Go jumped into his lap.

"I take it down when doctor say okay, okay?" He petted Go.

"Really?" This was the best piece of news I'd heard since we'd been here. "When?"

Daddy paused to think it over. "Maybe April."

"Oh." That wasn't soon enough.

"Is that all?" He looked at me as though he knew about Mayo and the Dare and my boy problems.

"Yup." I carefully wadded up the newspaper into tight little balls.

"Who's Tom?"

I gaped at him. "Who told you?"

"Your sister."

That insect.

"She say Tom your boyfriend." Daddy cleared his throat.

Uh-oh. The way he did that told me he was about to launch another attempt to explain *S-E-X*. I remembered the first time he tried. The lesson involved tadpoles and Alaskan salmon migration. I had to put a stop to this. "He's not my boyfriend."

Daddy pushed Go off his lap and clasped his hands. "I see."

Was it that obvious? That I was probably the only girl ever to garner a rejection from ... from ... *Brain-Damaged Boy*? I chucked a newspaper ball at my wastebasket. I missed.

Daddy sank to the carpet. "Girls grow up quicker than boys, Baby. You wait. They catch up." He looked at me ... really looked at me. "You're beautiful." He pinched my cheek, even though he knew I hated that. "Beautiful."

He put his arm around me, and I couldn't resist leaning against him. I put my hand over his heart. "You're not going to die, are you?"

Daddy gave me a squeeze and winked. "Not over my dead body."

chapter 15

The next morning at school, I had just gotten settled into my desk when Mayo walked in. The first words out of her mouth were, "We're on for tonight."

I forced some pep into my voice. "Excellent!"

While Mayo got something out of her backpack, I cast a furtive glance at Tom's empty chair, hoping he would be coming in today. I sighed when the bell rang and Mrs. Wembly began her lesson. But a moment later, my wish came true. The door opened and Tom walked in. His mother was right behind him, carrying his backpack. She started a conversation with our teacher.

My heart skipped as I studied Tom. He looked nice for someone who'd banged into a basketball post and landed himself in the hospital only days before. No bandages on his head or anything. Just his arm in a navy blue sling.

As he slid into his desk, I forced myself to remember we were *"just friends,"* but I couldn't stop the agony I felt when I glanced at his arm again, all wrapped up. Probably battered and bruised underneath. *Poor Tom.*

"Paris," Mayo whispered. "Quit it."

She had caught me looking at him.

"Mayo," Mrs. Wembly said, stopping Mrs. Cox mid-sentence. "Do you think this is an opportunity for chitchat?"

"No, ma'am."

I quickly dropped my gaze. I really had to stop thinking about him.

At lunch, Mayo didn't discuss the Dare. *For once.* I guessed she was saving it for our meeting at Dana's. Instead, we talked basketball. Dana gave me the run-down on tonight's team. The Calhoun Prairie Dogs were slightly below average, meaning some years, the Bumblebees would win, and other years, the Dogs would. Her only warning was, "Watch out for number fourteen, Stephanie Tenuta—you don't want to get in her way. The girl is bigger than a minivan." After school, we went back to Dana's for our big powwow over the Dare. Dana and I sat on her daybed while Mayo sorted through photocopies on the floor.

"Check this out." Mayo handed me a sheet of paper and sat next to me.

I read the headline: *Missing Birthday Girl Took Dare.* It featured an image of the woods by a swollen creek. A woman and man, who could only be Beth's parents, placed flowers on the scene. I skimmed the story. An unnamed boy confessed he challenged Beth Conlon to stay in the woods overnight on her thirteenth birthday. Mayo had highlighted the date—February 20, 1986. Every hair on my arm stood up.

"It's fate, Paris, fate!" Mayo said.

I nodded and tried to ignore the sinking feeling in my stomach. Maybe this time Mayo was right.

Mayo took the article from me before I could finish. "In this one," she said, "they hadn't found you-know-who yet. It just says they dredged Miller's Creek on the Conlon property. I betcha that's where the photo was taken."

"Have you seen the creek?" Dana asked.

I shook my head.

"And we found this." Mayo handed me another article. *Break in Conlon Case.* I scanned the text. After months of investigation, police had no more leads. No suspects. Until a hunter discovered human remains in the woods nearly two years after her disappearance. Near Miller's Creek, under a heavy log. I studied the picture of a dried-up creek bed and a tarp covering something. My insides knotted up.

"So did she drown or was it murder?" I asked.

"Well," Mayo said, "the rest of the articles say she probably drowned. They think maybe her body got trapped under a fallen log in the creek, and that's how the search party missed her. It wasn't until the dam for Sugar Lake was built that the creek dried up and the hunter came across her." She grinned at me. "And here's the juicy part. They only found 159 out of 206 bones. Makes you wonder where the rest is, huh?"

I swallowed.

Dana shuddered. "So there really could be a killer."

"Yup." Mayo pointed to another article. "According to

this one, foul play was never ruled out. Her death became a classic cold case. But here's what's disappointing. I can't pinpoint exactly where her remains were found. The articles only mention the creek's name. I found it on a map, but that's it. And there's nothing about finding dolls anywhere. You think people made that part up?"

"Um . . ." I pretended to read the article again. "Well . . ."

She squinted at me. "Well, what? You know something, don't you?"

"What is it, Paris?" Dana said.

Maybe sharing my experiences with my friends would get them so scared, they'd change their minds.

I doubted it. But I'd try anything. "I saw a doll."

"Are you for real?" Mayo said.

I nodded.

"Ohmigoodness!" Dana grabbed her pillow.

"This is unbelievable," Mayo exclaimed. "Where is it, what does it look like, where'd you find it?" She must have asked fifty questions at once. I wasn't sure. I was thinking about what I saw. Or didn't see.

"I was taking my dog out," I began. "It was still dark— early morning. And she had this . . . this . . . *thing* in her mouth." I measured the size with my hands. "About that big." Actually, I wasn't certain, but I figured bigger was better.

Dana gasped.

"What else?" Mayo said.

"A dress. White shoes? I was half asleep. It happened so fast."

"So where is it?"

"I don't know."

"Don't know?"

Dana held the pillow tight. "Did it disappear?!"

"Did you look for it?" Mayo asked.

I stared at her. "Are you nuts?!"

"Well, do you know where it might have come from?"

I thought about the spot by my window. How it had looked untouched. "No. Go just had it all of a sudden."

Mayo bit her lip, eyes darting back and forth. "Anything else? Have you seen anything else?"

"No . . ." But the concern in her voice got me going. Maybe this was working. "I have been hearing more things, though."

"More things?" Mayo said. "What things? You never mentioned this before."

Suddenly I realized I had only told Dana about them at the library. *Shoot.* Dana gave me a look, but didn't say anything. "Well, I never thought it was worth mentioning," I lied. "I mean, the sounds could have been anything, really."

"What were they?" Mayo said.

"First it was laughing, then it was tapping, and just the other day, voices . . ."

"Voices?!" Dana blurted.

I nodded. "A boy and a girl. Girl mostly. I couldn't understand any of it. But the girl was mad!" I checked Mayo for a reaction. That ought to scare her good.

Mayo's eyes were about as big as Dana's now. "That

does it. This fits right into what I was thinking last night . . ." She got off the bed, taking the articles with her. "I've had my doubts about you-know-what . . ."

Was she changing her mind?

Mayo opened her backpack on the floor. "No, we can't do it . . ." She put the articles inside.

Dana and I let out a breath. If I had known it was this easy, I would have confessed to my insanity ages ago.

"Not this way," Mayo interrupted. "We have to take this one step further." She pulled out a book and flipped through it.

I read the title. *"Ten Ways to Talk to Your Dead One?!"*

"I took it from Roxy. I thought it might make our evening more entertaining."

"Entertaining?" Dana grimaced.

I groaned and flopped backward onto the bed.

Mayo read from a page and lowered her voice. "'Number one: When a dead person talks, you must listen. Spirits may not have the power to vocalize like mortals do. But they can leave clues. Clues to their existence. Heed these signs and talk back!'"

"What?!" I said.

Words spilled out of her. "Don't you get it? You-know-who is practically telling us to take the Dare for her. All those sounds you've been hearing? The voices? She's trying to communicate. The doll has to be a sign from her, too. It's a *manifestation,* a physical representation of the spiritual!" She hugged the book to her chest and looked up at the ceiling. "Isn't this awesome?"

Dana and I glanced at each other. Then Dana said, "Yeah. Awesome!"

But I couldn't bring myself to say the same.

"So, Mayo, what are we supposed to do next?" Dana said.

"We have to let her know we're receiving her messages, of course."

"Oh yeah?" I raised my eyebrows. "How?"

Mayo leaned in. "Have you ever heard of a Ouija board? The book says it's the simplest way to get a conversation going."

Dana wrinkled her face. *"Weegee?"*

"I know what it is." I thought back to when I played the one Athens got for Christmas years ago. You set a pointer on a board that has all the letters of the alphabet on it. Then you put your fingers on the pointer and eventually it spells out messages from spirits. My brother never used it, but I did. I freaked out Verona for weeks when I revealed her Barbie liked her hair done up straight, not curly. *Wait a second . . .*

"I've got one, Mayo."

She lit up. "You do?"

"Uh-huh."

She held out her hand for a high five.

I slapped it hard.

Dana didn't look too pleased with me.

But I ignored her and smiled.

"This *is* fate, Paris," Mayo said. "I was thinking we might have to get Roxy to order one on eBay—"

"But what's you-know-who going to tell us?" Dana interrupted.

"Where we're supposed to go in the woods, of course," Mayo replied. "And I have a few other ideas."

So did I.

In fact, I knew exactly what Beth would tell us.

Anything I wanted.

Before we left for the game, we decided we'd do Ouija as soon as possible—tomorrow after dinner—seven. I was so happy about my idea, I didn't even mind basketball that night. Even when Verona and the Honeys belly-danced to some Indian techno song during halftime. Even when I accidentally got in Stephanie Tenuta's way and she steamrolled right over me.

After the game, Athens took Verona and me home. When we stepped in, our house smelled great—like someone had grilled burgers or something. Daddy called to us from the dining room. "Hey, everybody. Where you all go? I make dinner and no one here."

"Basketball," Athens said.

Verona slipped off her shoes. "Where's Mom?"

"She work," Daddy replied.

Now there's a shocker. I dumped my backpack on the floor, then started tugging off my jacket.

"So there was game tonight, huh?" my father said.

"Yeah, Daddy." Verona headed to the dining room.

Athens kicked off his sneakers. "Mom didn't tell you?"

I stared at Athens and cocked my head. *"Mom?"* As far

as I knew, he was still grounded. Why didn't *he* tell Daddy before he picked us up. "Athens, how come you—"

My brother glared at me. "Be quiet, Paris," he whispered. "I'll take Go out for another week."

"Deal," I whispered back. "So, Daddy," I said loudly. "How come you didn't tell us you were making dinner?" Even though I had grabbed a quick bite at Dana's, I could definitely eat something. I joined him by the table.

"It's surprise," my father said. "I make nachos. Daddy style."

It was Daddy style, all right. The table was set up like an all-you-can-eat buffet. "Do you really think you should be having this?"

Athens gave me a look.

"What?" I said.

Verona shook her head. "Don't you know you can't change him, Paris?"

"Baby, don't worry about me." Daddy scooped a bunch of Tostitos onto his plate. "This is well-balanced meal. We've got onions, tomatoes, lettuce . . ."

"And meat and cheese and sour cream . . ." I added.

"Like I said," my father replied, "well balanced." He spooned up a huge helping of ground beef and spread it all over his plate of chips. "*Please, Baby.* You eat your food. I eat mine. Now we all sit and talk. I want to say something important."

I took my seat, then held back a groan when my father reached for the nacho cheese.

"What did you want to talk about, Daddy?" Verona said.

"Your mom."

I scrunched my forehead. "What's wrong with her?"

"Nothing wrong. Just want to say that now we don't move, things be different. Your mother work extra hard until Hank and I finish house in Choctaw. Then we sell house and your daddy find job here. Though I don't know what I do . . . Maybe I turn these twenty acres into big subdivision. But that will take more money . . . SO . . ." He popped a fully loaded chip into his mouth and chewed while he spoke. "Be good. Listen to Mom. She under a lot of pressure, okay?"

"Sure, Daddy," Verona said.

"Fine," Athens mumbled.

I didn't say anything.

"Baby?"

"What?"

"You be good, too, right?"

I nodded, but all I could think was, *What about you*? I watched him dredge another chip through meat, cheese, and sour cream—forget the tomatoes.

Was *he* being good?

chapter 16

I got up with a positive attitude the next morning. Despite my father's flagrant ignorance of his health, I still had something to be happy about. If things went my way with Ouija tonight, I'd be in good shape for the Dare. I even found it in me to take my father's advice and be extra good to my mother. After I ate breakfast, I stopped by my parents' bedroom to wish her a good day as she got ready for work. But I was surprised to see her still in bed. Daddy was snoring beside her. "Mom?" I whispered. "Why are you still sleeping?"

My mother pulled her blankets up to her chin. "Wha?" She didn't open her eyes.

"Mom, are you sick?"

"No," she mumbled. "Boss let me go to work late today. I got home two a.m. last night."

I left the room with a sigh. I felt bad for her. How much longer could she keep it up?

I went back to my room, and just as I was packing my backpack, my door slammed against the wall. "Paris!" Athens barked.

I slipped my notebook into my backpack. "What?!"

"Don't leave your toys where Go can get ahold of them."

Something covered in dirt thudded onto my desk.

A doll was facedown in front of me, wearing white shoes and a patterned dress.

I didn't move. *It's real.*

Go put her paws on my knees.

"I had to pry this from her mouth," Athens continued.

Another item thunked onto my desk. The doll's arm.

Go panted at me. My door slammed shut.

HOLY COW. I leapt out of my chair and burst into the hall. "ATHENNNNNS!"

"What?"

"Where did Go get that *thing*?"

"Heck if I know," he said. "I wasn't monitoring her every move. In the yard somewhere. Now get Verona and be at the car in five."

He shut the door.

I turned around slowly, then stared at the door to my room. Maybe I should have never said anything about finding a doll. Maybe you-know-who had been listening. Maybe she *was* trying to communicate—*Stop it, Paris! For the last time, you don't believe in ghosts!*

I steeled myself and pushed open my door.

The doll was resting on my desk exactly where I'd left it. Facedown.

I went to my desk.

Brown ringlets. A muddied-up floral smock. I nudged it with my pen. It didn't nudge back. GOOD THING.

Now flip it over. All right, that's it.

I turned the doll onto its back.

Oh, man!

The doll had a china face. And it was cracked down the middle. I shivered.

I ran through the idea of telling Daddy but quickly dismissed it. *You found a doll, Baby? Good, good. Have fun!*

What about Mayo and Dana?

I could hear Mayo already. *This is fate, Paris, FATE!*

Gritting my teeth, I removed the thing (and its arm) from my desk as though it was nothing more than what it was—a toy. When Go saw the doll come down, she pawed at my jeans. I ignored her, reached under my bed, and grabbed my violin case.

I took out my instrument, put the doll and its limb into the case, and snapped the buckles shut.

Get yourself out of that!

I carried the case to my closet and shut the door.

I felt better.

I scooted my desk chair under the doorknob.

Much better.

At school, all I thought about was how much I wanted to tell Tom about what I had in my closet. He looked my way a few times, but he could have been staring at the world map behind me for all I knew. *Ugh.* Of course, at lunch this time, all Mayo focused on was Ouija, Ouija, Ouija. And practice was more of the same plus one unexpected bonk to the head. By the end of the day, I wondered why I had even been happy this morning.

Things didn't get any better when I got home. I swiped

about fifty pounds of junk food from my father, and I spent my last hour before my friends arrived sitting on my bed—as far away from my closet as possible—while I planned what would happen during a rousing game of Ouija. Just as I'd figured it all out, my door banged against the wall.

"Paris," Verona said.

I glared at her. "Can't you knock?"

She stepped in, wearing her basketball uniform. What was she doing in that? "Mom said your dork friends are coming over soon."

"So?"

"Keep it down, or else. My friends are coming over, too. We're practicing tonight."

Great. The last thing I needed was to hear Verona and four other airheads cheering from the next room. "Practicing what?" I said. "Don't you have stupid covered already?"

Verona narrowed her eyes. *"Just be quiet."* She strutted out.

When Mayo and Dana showed up at my front door, I pulled them to my room before my parents had a chance to humiliate me. I got the Ouija board out from under my bed.

"Wait." Mayo stopped me. She grabbed my desk chair and pushed it against my bedroom door.

I stared at my closet without its barricade and tried to act casual.

Next Mayo tugged the blanket off my bed, and Dana helped her tie one end to my bedpost and the other to my desk, forming a perfect barrier between us and the door.

"For privacy," Mayo said, admiring her work. She opened her backpack and whipped out a notepad and a pen. "You got the candles and the lighter, Dana?"

Dana nodded and took three pillars from her bag.

I set the pointer onto the Ouija board. Mayo brought down some books from my shelf and rested the candles on them. Dana lit them.

"Paris, get the lights," Mayo said.

My room was now perfect séance headquarters.

"One more thing." Mayo pulled out *Ten Ways to Talk to Your Dead One*. "We've got to do this right." She flipped it to a page and read by the candlelight. "'When participants are gathered together to summon the deceased, ensure each person is fully open and willing to communicate. It is helpful to begin with an invitation, statements spoken aloud in the manner of a friendly greeting, such as—insert dead person's name—we are gathered to hear you. We come with open minds. Speak with us now.'"

Mayo lowered the book. "Come on," she whispered. "Say it."

"Beth, we are gathered to hear you . . ."

I'd never thought I'd hate a book, but I did now.

When we finished, Mayo continued. "'It is particularly

helpful to bring an object that was once in the deceased's possession or, though not as effective, a photo of the deceased.'" She glanced up. "I brought that article with Beth's picture in it for this part."

I glanced in the direction of the closet. I didn't think we needed that.

I listened to Mayo read about "relevant objects." How spirits and those objects were drawn to each other through paranormal energy. Hearing this made me think of the dark insides of my closet. Despite what I thought about ghosts, I imagined Beth—huddled in the shadows, holding the doll.

Chills ran through me.

Mayo went on. "Make sure you always keep at least one hand on the pointer. It says if you let go when a spirit's communicating, you may become possessed."

Possessed? I swallowed. The image of Beth still lingered in my mind. *Quit it, Paris. No one is getting possessed.*

"Now I'll ask the questions." Mayo set the notepad in her lap and held the pen. She rested her free hand on the pointer. "Ready?"

Dana's and my fingers joined Mayo's on the disk.

I concentrated on my hands and channeled all of my energy into them. I couldn't mess this up.

Mayo began. "Beth Conlon, are you here?"

I counted to three and pushed the disk slowly . . . So far, so good.

"Ohmigoodness," Dana whispered.

"Shhh," Mayo said. "Don't scare Beth away."

I let the pointer rest at *Yes*.

Dana gasped.

"Beth," Mayo said, "tell us where to go."

Where to go? "Why don't you ask if she wants us to do the Dare first?" I said. The conversation would go quicker that way: NO.

"Paris, be quiet. She could leave us any second. No time for obvious questions."

I sighed as I stared at our hands.

"Beth," Mayo repeated, "tell us where to go."

This was it. The long answer. I inched the pointer.

"What's happening?" Dana looked at Mayo. "What's she saying?"

"Be patient, Dana. Beth's getting to it. There it is—the first letter. *S!*" Mayo scribbled down the letter.

I inched toward my second letter.

"*T,*" Dana said.

My third letter. "*A.*" My confidence grew.

When I finished the entire message, I didn't know why I was even worried.

Mayo read from her notepad. "*Stay home?*"

I feigned surprise. It was a great look; I had practiced it in the mirror a hundred times.

"Why is Beth saying that?" Dana said.

Mayo's forehead wrinkled. "Let me think."

Dana fidgeted.

"Don't let go," Mayo warned.

Dana froze.

"I think I know what's happening," Mayo said. "Beth wouldn't say that."

No way. "You don't believe what the dead girl tells you?" I said. "Isn't that traitorous?"

"Paris, listen to me—it's not her. No spirit would tell us to stay at home if we're supposed to solve her mystery. That doesn't make any sense. The book warned me about this. Sometimes when you open a portal, you get evil spirits. Chapter four: 'The Good, the Dead, and the Ugly.'"

Dana's fingers trembled on the disk. So did mine.

"Tell me who you are," Mayo said. She glanced at both of us. "Whatever you do . . . Don't. Let. Go."

We stared at the pointer.

Bang!

We yelped and jerked our hands back. I heard my chair crash against something.

"Paris!" Verona snapped, tearing down the blanket. "What are you doing?"

My chair was in front of her, and the closet door was cracked open. *What the?*

"*Ouija?*" my sister said. "Haven't you grown out of that by now? We're about to rehearse our cheer, and all we hear is you all gabbing. Shut up!" She stomped out.

Mayo closed my bedroom door. "Do you feel possessed?"

All I could do was focus on the closet. I kept seeing Beth in my mind. *Shut the closet.*

"Paris?" Dana shook me.

"Shut the closet!" I said.

I leapt to my feet, pushed the chair out of the way, and did it myself.

"Mayo," Dana whispered, "what's wrong with her?"

Mayo pointed at the closet. "What's in there, Paris?"

I leaned against the door. "Nothing."

She pushed me aside and flung the closet open.

I let out a huge breath. It was just my violin case. *Thank goodness.*

Mayo looked from me to my case. She reached for it.

"Don't, Mayo."

"What are you hiding?"

She set the case on my bed.

"Uh . . . it's nothing."

"Well, if it's nothing," Mayo said, "then what's the big deal?" She undid the latches.

I looked away.

"It's just a violin," Mayo said.

chapter 17

I looked at the case, then scanned the room. "Where's the doll?"

"*Doll?*" Mayo said.

Oh, man. Did I say that out loud?

Mayo pointed to the case. "You had a doll in here?!"

"No!" My heart raced. *Where did it go?*

"Well, then . . . what? . . ." Mayo covered her mouth. "Holy smokes, another manifestation."

Dana scooted next to me and clung to my arm. "That doesn't sound good. Is it still here?"

"Mayo, search the room. Find it." I huddled with Dana.

"Find it?" Mayo only stood there. "I'm not going to be able to find it. It was a vision, Paris. And now you've had two of them!"

I wished she'd stop reminding me and just look for the creepy doll.

"Mayo, please!" Dana begged. She buried her face in my shoulder.

"You all have got to be kidding me," Mayo said.

We shook our heads.

"Fine, I'll look, but this is totally pointless." She went to the closet and rummaged inside. "I'm not going to find anything." She lifted up my bed skirt. "Nothing. See?" She checked my nightstand and dumped out my trash can. "It's all clear. Now will you listen to me?"

I started to breathe again. Dana loosened her grip.

"I think I know what's going on." Mayo picked her book off the floor and thumbed through the pages. "You say you've been hearing noises and voices, right? A girl and a boy?"

"Yeah," I said, "but you're not going to find the answers in that book." No, there had to be a logical explanation for everything, including the vanishing doll. Who would have taken it and put my violin back?

"Yup, it's all here," Mayo said. "Chapter twelve: 'Dial the Dead Direct . . .'"

Mom. It had to be her. But wouldn't she have torn into me about leaving out a six-hundred-dollar violin and dirtying up a two-hundred-dollar case—"We don't have eight hundred dollar here, eight hundred dollar there!"— It didn't make sense.

Mayo thrust the book in my face. "Paris Pan, you are a medium. *You* can communicate with the dead!"

"Ohmigoodness," Dana said.

"Please." I pushed away the book and started putting up the Ouija board. "I am not a medium."

But Mayo wouldn't let it go. She went on and on about how I had to be a clairvoyant. Like those people who help the police solve cold cases using only a photo or a scrap of clothes as a clue. While she talked, I thought about the noises and the doll and drew a couple of conclusions. The sounds were probably hallucinations conjured by my sick mind. And the doll? That had to be real—not some message from you-know-who. I touched it. Go chewed on it. But more importantly, Athens had brought it in.

"Paris, why don't you believe me?"

"I'll tell you why. There's no science behind this medium-ghost stuff."

"Yes, there is. There's plenty of science behind it."

"Yeah, right."

Mayo grabbed the book. "This thing has a fancy reference list in the back and footnotes everywhere. It's all here. Read it and you'll see."

"But I don't get it," Dana said. "If Beth is talking to Paris, then wouldn't Beth have been the one speaking during Ouija? Telling us to stay home? Maybe we shouldn't do you-know-what."

Good thinking, Dana. I nodded emphatically. "Yeah."

"Nope," Mayo replied. "Ouija is different. You could get anyone with that thing. Remember what I said about evil spirits? I know who it was."

I bet she did.

"Who?" Dana asked.

"The killer, of course."

I groaned.

"Who else would want us to stay at home?" Mayo said. "He's afraid if we go into those woods and figure out exactly what happened to you-know-who, his awful truth will be exposed to the world. It all fits."

"What fits?"

"The sounds, the voices . . . I bet you a million bucks Beth is replaying the night of her murder. I mean, the part about hearing a girl and a boy arguing? It makes me wonder if the killer was actually the kid who dared Beth—"

"No way," Dana said.

"Maybe they got into a fight that night. Or maybe he accidentally hurt her and covered it up. Let's think about it. The police would hardly suspect it was just a kid. It all has to tie together somehow."

I frowned—someone *our* age? A killer?

Wait a second. I stared at the *Psychology Today* book that was under one of the candles. What had I read about antisocial personality disorder? *It typically presents itself during childhood.* My throat went dry. That would put the killer in his thirties now. He'd still have plenty of pep left in him if he was still around. *What if Mayo is actually on to something?*

"Well, don't look so upset, Paris," Mayo said. "This is *good* news!"

"Good news?" Dana and I said.

"Don't you get it? We have nothing to worry about. If the murderer's speaking to us through the Ouija board, he must be dead, too."

"But . . ." I wanted to tell her it was just me pushing the pointer, but I knew I had to play along. ". . . Um, wouldn't that mean the boy died kinda young?"

"Yeah, and *so?* Do you think after doing something like that, he would die of natural causes? *Please.* He probably died prematurely from guilt."

Oh, brother.

"Look, it's just a theory. Who knows what really happened? All I know is that whoever was talking to us during Ouija was someone who doesn't want us to find out the truth."

I didn't respond. I was too busy sorting out my jumbled thoughts about Beth, the Dare, ghosts, mental disorders, mediums, and now child killers?! . . . I was starting to get a headache.

"Yes, things are going our way, girls. Fate has been kind to us." Mayo looked at me. "Now that we've got you, I'm confident we're going to solve this mystery once and for all. Here." She passed me the book.

"What do you want me to do with this?"

"Read it, duh. The book said mediums can hone their talents. Seeing dolls is just the beginning! You've got two days."

"To do what?"

"Find out where we're supposed to go in those woods, and if you get more out of her, I won't complain!"

While Mayo smiled at me, I gripped the book. Two days.

Two days to figure out what the heck was going on.

● ● ●

After Mayo and Dana left, I got ready for bed, then sat at my desk. I drew up a chart for my investigation:

FIGURE OUT WHAT HAPPENED TO THE DOLL

Step 1. Confirm the doll's existence first.

    A. Search my violin case for physical signs left by the doll.

    B. Talk to Athens. Affirm he once had the doll in his possession.

Step 2. Carefully feel out Mom for indications she took the doll and miraculously forgot to dole out a punishment.

Step 3. If no luck there, check myself into a psycho ward.

I spun in my chair. My violin case was still open on my bed. It was time for step 1A.

I set Go next to the case. "Sniff," I ordered.

She looked at the case, lay down, and rested her chin on her paws.

I thought she'd pick up a scent and go nuts over it. Maybe it had been too long.

Fine. I'd have to inspect the case myself.

I pulled a magnifying glass from my desk drawer and went over the inside of the lid. Nothing.

I lifted out the violin. Surely, the doll would have left a trace. Maybe a hair. A fleck of mud. I peered at the felt lining. It was clean. I checked the rosin compartment. Clear.

As I crossed 1A off the list, hopelessness welled up within me.

I glanced at Mayo's book on my desk. Maybe she was right.

Nah.

I still had 1B.

I headed for Athens's room and knocked.

My brother grumbled, "Who is it?"

"Me."

More grumbling. "Enter."

I opened the door and walked in. Athens was sitting at his desk, looking like he'd slept in his clothes, his hair sticking up at all angles. The blinds were down, and his lamp was on.

"What do you want?" He was bent over yet another application.

I sat on the edge of Athens's bed. "I seem to have misplaced my doll." I folded my hands in my lap and twiddled my thumbs. "Do you know where it might be?"

My brother's back stiffened. He couldn't have been comfortable hunched over like that. "What doll?" he said. "And why should I care?"

"You know, the one you threw in my room this morning."

Athens rubbed his neck and gave it a crack. "I have no idea what you're talking about." He went back to his application.

I stood up. "Yeah, you do. Don't you remember? *You threw it in my room.*"

"No, I didn't."

What? "You did, too."

"Paris"—he stopped writing—"you're starting to get on my nerves. Can't you see I'm in the middle of something?"

"But—"

"Don't make me turn around."

"But . . ." I said it quietly this time.

"Paris!"

"Fine." I marched to the door. "I know you're lying." He had to be.

"Wait," Athens said.

I stopped and looked at him.

My brother leaned back and studied me. "Is there something you want to tell me?"

I crossed my arms as though doing so would cover up all my problems. "No."

He raised an eyebrow. "You sure? You've been acting kind of funny lately."

"Oh, really?" I snapped. "Since when have you noticed anything about me at all?"

My brother put up his hands. "Jeez, forget I asked."

I spun on my heels and shut the door.

I couldn't believe my brother had the nerve to think I had something to tell him when *he* was the liar. I started down the hall. But why would he lie about the doll? Why would he lie about something like that?

With each step toward my bedroom, my resolve dwindled. I turned in the hall and glanced at Athens's door. I tried to imagine myself telling him everything. He used to listen to me, give me advice. Now? I couldn't picture it. He was a different person and so was I.

Maybe *I* had outgrown *him*.

When I reached my desk, I studied the cover of Mayo's book. *Ten Ways to Talk to Your Dead One*, by Dr. T. R. Smith, Ph.D.

Was everything I had experienced really made up in my head?

Or was *someone* trying to communicate?

I didn't know.

I turned to the back of the book. A whole bibliography like Mayo had said.

This had to be the longest day of my entire life.

I carried the book to my bed, snuggled with Go, and opened it to page one.

chapter 18

That night, I got through only a quarter of the book. So far, it covered stuff like how to hold a séance, how to tell if your psychic is a fraud, and common ways the deceased communicate. I concluded I had experienced a lot of them: (1) sounds, (2) visions, (3) dreams, (4) presentation of physical objects, (5) disappearance of physical objects. The only things I hadn't experienced were (6) written messages, (7) seeing the actual spirit, and (8) being lifted off the ground.

I had so much to look forward to.

By the time I called it quits, I felt like I really wasn't crazy in the conventional sense of the word. In chapter five, "Tools for Ghouls," I read an extensive explanation of the equipment used to detect paranormal activity— electromagnetic field detectors, special audio recording equipment, and infrared thermometers. I closed the book and rubbed my eyes. Maybe there was some science behind this stuff.

I got back into bed and put on my earmuffs.

Maybe ghosts did exist.

I stared at my window and shuddered.

At lunch the next day, Mayo was already on my case

about my *clairvoyancy.* "So?" she said. "Got anything from Beth?"

I sighed. "No. I haven't even gotten to the part in the book about mediums yet."

Dana looked relieved.

"Hurry up, then," Mayo said. "The clock is ticking. After tomorrow, it's D-day."

"I know."

"Well, while we're waiting on *you*"—Mayo straightened— "let's go over a couple more things in preparation for our little adventure." She slipped out a green glow stick from her pocket.

"What's that for?" Dana said.

Mayo flipped the stick in her hands. "This was my survival strategy. I've got a ton of Halloween leftovers. Once you break them, they glow for hours. I thought we'd drop them as we go so we could find our way back."

Survival strategy? I was surprised she even cared about living afterward. "Good thinking, Mayo. Bring as many as you got."

"One more order of business," Mayo said. "Dana and I are carpooling to the game on Saturday and then back to your house. You want to ride with us?"

"Game? There's a game on Saturday, too?" She had to be kidding me.

"Paris," Dana said, "don't you hear anything Coach Dobson says? We're playing the Washington Giants. It's the biggest game of the year!"

"I must be too busy trying to stay alive during practice." This was just great. A game and the Dare in the same night. I must be the luckiest person alive.

"So you need a ride or what?" Mayo asked.

"No." I sighed. "I'm sure Athens will be happy to take me."

When I got home from practice, I grabbed Mayo's book. After a couple more unsettling chapters about the reasons behind ghost hauntings—unexpected death, wrongful death, and just plain evilness—I finally got to chapter twelve: "Dial the Dead Direct."

I learned some people are born with a sixth sense, a.k.a. extrasensory perception (ESP). Others train for months, even years, to develop it. I came to a self-assessment quiz that determined if my ESP fell within the range of mediumship.

1. *Do you know who is on the other end of the phone before you pick it up?* I thought about my sister. Uh-huh.
2. *Have you had déjà vu?* Every time I see a moving truck.
3. *Do you often associate a terrible history with seemingly harmless objects?*

I swallowed.

Mom called us to dinner, and I couldn't wait to put the book down.

When I got to the dining room, everyone was taking their places behind their rice bowls. I sat and nudged a plate of cabbage toward my father. Mom set out the rest of the meal.

"Sweet and sour pork?!" I gasped. "Eggs?!"

"Bok choy is Daddy's," Mom replied.

My father's chopsticks headed for the meat anyway.

I looked from my sister to my brother to my mother. No one seemed to care. I couldn't just watch Daddy go for a second heart attack. I had to do something.

I gripped his wrist. "You heard Mom," I said. "Drop it."

My siblings sighed.

"Baby," Daddy said, "this Chinese food, okay? Good for me."

I doubted a plate of fat and a gigantic bowl of steamed cholesterol was good for him.

"Come off it, Paris," Verona whispered.

"This is getting old," Athens muttered.

I wouldn't let go.

"Daughter . . ." Daddy lost his smile. "I'm father, remember?"

I released him. "Not for long," I whispered.

"Wha?" He shoved a glob of pork into his mouth.

"Nothing."

Mom gave me the same old tired look as she laid food into my bowl. "Your daddy thinks he better than doctor, remember?" She looked sideways at my father. "Let him eat."

Oh, good. Mom was mad at him, too.

"Doro-see," Daddy said, "children here. We all here.

Let's talk like family. Let's talk dreams, wishes, *plans,* huh? When last time we do that?"

Athens, Verona, and I rolled our eyes at the same time.

"Son, you oldest. You start."

"Plans?" Athens said as he worked down his rice. "Get into college and leave town quickly." The last part didn't come out so loudly, but I heard it.

Daddy put his hand to his ear. "Wha? Speak up."

"I said," Athens repeated, "get into U.C. Berkeley."

"Good, good." Daddy smiled. "My son know what he doing. You hear that, Wa-wa, Baby? Berkeley. Top-notch school. Now who next?"

I stared at him as he put another piece of meat in his mouth. "Me, Daddy." I knew exactly what I wanted to say.

"See?" My father wagged his chopsticks at Verona. "Baby good girl. She volunteer. Tell me what you want to do."

"Stop Daddy from dying."

Mom dropped her bowl and chopsticks. "Baby, go to your room!"

"But it's the truth!" I mean, there were other options, like stop the Dare, but the one I had chosen was equally accurate. "Mom, you can't punish me for being honest. Besides, you're the one who said Daddy should keep eating!"

"Baby!" Her hand smacked the table.

I flinched, but I didn't budge. I was so tired of this.

"What do you want to happen, Mom?" I stood up. "You want Daddy to die right in front of us?"

"Baby!" My father's face turned red like he wasn't getting any oxygen.

Oh, man. What had I done?

"Daddy, are you okay?"

"*Sit.* You don't talk to Mother this way!"

I sank into my chair. Athens and Verona gave me dirty looks.

Mom rested her forehead in her hands. "No, Frank. It's okay." Her voice got very quiet. "No one listens to Mother."

Verona kicked me from under the table.

Then my mother's shoulders started to shake.

"Mom?" I placed a hand on her arm.

She pushed me away and left the table. Daddy followed. "Doro-see."

I heard a door shut.

"Now look what you've done." Athens got up. "Dad told you mom was stressed out. And you go and make her cry. Good job, Paris."

Verona pushed back from the table. "You are dumber than dumb."

I stared at my bowl filled to the brim with Mom's cooking.

My sister was right.

● ● ●

Back in my room, I threw myself onto the bed and landed next to Mayo's book. I slid it under my pillow. I couldn't think about that now. I heard my brother yelling from the hallway. "I'm going to the library! Need to finish my applications!"

Yeah, right. At this hour? The library was closed. But I bet Mom, in her current state, wouldn't notice he was leaving. Or the fact that it was a violation of his grounding.

Someone knocked on my door. "Baby?"

It was Daddy.

"Can't you tell I'm sleeping?"

He came in anyway. I flipped onto my side and faced the wall.

"Baby?" I heard Daddy roll my chair over.

He wasn't getting anything out of me.

"You mad at me, too. Is that it?"

Bingo.

"You like your mother. Worry all the time. Not good for you."

I let out a long breath.

"I tell your mom, she with you children every day. It's blessing!"

I buried my face into my pillow. What did this have to do with anything?

"I say I miss everything. You know what? Mom just say same thing."

Surprise, surprise.

"We work, then we worry so Athens, and Wa-wa, and

you can go to good school and have good future. Now . . ." I heard him sigh. "Athens all grown up."

Daddy paused, and something wrapped itself tight around my heart. "But your father think, this is what we want—what we work for. So maybe you all don't be like your mom and me. Work so hard for what? Right?"

I nodded.

"And when I get sick. I say, Lord, what you trying to tell me? And I think maybe He say, 'Daddy, stop moving!' Where else I go with heart like this? But now I learn this is only half of answer."

"Half?" I rolled onto my back and looked at him—sagging in my chair, talking more to his folded hands than to me.

"You're right. I should take care myself. I *will* take care myself." He shook his head. "*Ay-yuh*, your daddy like donkey. Drag and pull and yell and still don't go anywhere. You forgive me?"

I sat up. "Well . . ." I put an expression on my face that made me look like I was thinking hard about it.

"You daddy now, huh?"

I smiled.

He held out his arms.

As we hugged, I asked, "Is Mom okay?"

"Your mom need rest. She fine, you see."

After Daddy left, I chose to believe him about Mom. The woman really could use a nap. I sighed as I tried to put her out of my mind. I grabbed Mayo's book from under my pillow. As if on cue, hip-hop beats started wafting through the wall from Verona's room. I draped my comforter over my head and dragged Go in with me. I turned on Daddy's flashlight. I read what was next in the book. *If you answered yes to all three questions in the quiz, congratulations, you could be a medium.*

Great.

I read on and reached a do-it-yourself portion for contacting the deceased. *Welcome, Medium. If this is your first attempt at communicating with the otherworld, please note, results do vary. Good luck!*

I poked my head out of the covers for some air. There was no way I was going to channel the dead no matter what Mayo said.

Eeeeeeeer.

I glanced at the window.

All right. Let me rethink that.

I scooted back under my blanket and continued reading. The book listed the key requirements that must be fulfilled to act as a medium.

Now I heard a voice. I tensed. A girl barely audible over Verona's music. Go growled beside me. I thought about what Mayo had said. Beth replaying the night of her murder. I tried to keep reading, but I couldn't take in the words.

The voice grew agitated, then stopped. Go pushed her way out of the covers and her growling grew louder. But she couldn't drown out another voice—a boy. I gulped.

Was Mayo right? Had he killed her? I shook my head. No, Beth drowned. *She drowned.* But Tom had suspected a murderer, too.

Suddenly, Go started barking like crazy. I had to look.

I threw back the covers.

Go was bouncing up and down in front of my window, yapping at nothing.

Then something flashed by.

Holy cow.

I squeezed my eyes shut as I pulled the covers over my head. *Bang!* I cringed. *The shed.*

Verona's music turned off.

She pounded on the wall. "Will you shut Go up?!"

Go's barks wound down to a whine.

I looked down at the book. *Forget this!* I shoved it off my bed and snapped on my earmuffs. I chanted in my head, *There's no such thing as a ghost, there's no such thing as a ghost. . . .*

But deep down, I knew something happened in that shed.

And Beth wouldn't stop until I knew what it was.

chapter 19

The next morning arrived as though nothing had ever happened. My room filled with light. I even thought I might have heard a bird chirping. Go was snuggled up under my arm. Her sleep was deep, brows not even twitching.

I got off my bed and inched toward the window. I made out the rotten boards of the shed among the branches. The door was closed.

I fumbled for the cord and dropped the blinds.

I still had an hour before I had to leave for school. In the shower, I figured out what to do about the sounds I'd heard. This took all of two seconds. I could go to the shed and serve myself up for the biggest scare of my life, or I could pretend I wasn't interested in what anyone had to say. *Because* . . . I thought of Mayo's book . . . *you can't talk to the dead if you refuse to listen.*

I needed to focus on my highest priority—the Dare. At this point, I didn't know how to stop it, but I wasn't about to get lost in the woods and starve while the search team overlooked my body. Nor was I going to commune with the dead or even chance a meeting with a killer making a comeback. I had to think of something good, something convincing, something that would preserve my life . . . yet maintain my key friendships. At last, I hammered in the final details of a three-step plan. It was risky, but it was all I had.

I executed step one by writing a note to Tom.

Instructions for You-Know-What

1. *Plant doll in woods near my house. Make it convincing. I would do it myself but (a) I've only got Sesame Street characters. And (b) I'm not fond of extra trips to the woods. If you buy one, I'll pay you back. Free math homework for the rest of the year!*
2. *Stay out there as backup. But don't be seen. THAT'S VERY IMPORTANT.*
3. *Meet me at fishing shack to discuss the details. Tonight, 5:00.*
4. *Destroy this note.*

I folded the note and reminded myself that from this point on, I was strictly a professional. Tom might not like me the same way I did him, but I hoped when he said friends, he meant it.

Right before I had to leave for school, I heard knocking at my door. I was confused by the foreign sound. Maybe it was Daddy? I shut my notebook and turned. "Come in."

It was Mom, looking way better than I thought she would after yesterday. She was dressed for work, her hair was done, and she had makeup on and everything. "Baby," she said, "I want to talk about last night."

I set down my pen. This would be fun. "But Daddy already did."

My mother sat on my bed. "You should hear from me."

"Fine," I said. But I already knew what she wanted to tell me. *What kind of daughter I have? Never yell at me. You grounded!* The only question I had was, for how long?

"I want to say I'm sorry," Mom said.

Whoa. Hang on. *Mom* was apologizing to *me*?

She smoothed her hair. "I shouldn't cry in front of you children. I'm your mother . . ."

I didn't say anything. I knew there had to be more because of the way she was acting. *Strange.*

"It's just your daddy always say one thing," Mom continued, "then do another."

Now I was confused. "He said he was going to change, though."

"Yes," Mom said, "but I wonder if my children have same problem, too." She gave me a standard issue *Mom* look.

I wrinkled my face. "What do you mean?"

"I don't know. You tell me."

For a second, I thought she might know about the Dare. But as soon as that entered my mind, I dismissed it. Like my mother would know what I was up to. "Sorry, Mom. I've got nothing for you," I lied. "What you see is what you get."

My mother continued to stare at me. "Are you sure?"

"Yup." I even smiled.

"All right." She stood up. "But now you know, I have new policy—longer kids keep truth from Mother, longer kids grounded. Got it?"

"Got it." But I wondered how that was different from her old policy.

When I got to school, I completed step two by dropping off Tom's message in the tree. Then I executed the final step at lunch when Mayo gave me the perfect lead-in. She didn't wait for me to sit down before she started blabbing about the Dare. "Tell me you got something from you-know-who today."

I sat beside her on the steps. "As a matter of fact, I did." I pulled a banana from my lunch sack and let step three roll right out of my mouth. "Miller's Creek is a false lead."

"A false lead?" Mayo said.

"What do you mean?" Dana asked.

"You-know-who is trying to tell me it happened some-where around my house."

Mayo looked at me funny. "Sounds a little convenient."

I raised my brows. "If that's what you want to believe . . ." I casually peeled my banana—a display of my confidence in my plan. "I'd be happy to tell you-know-who how you feel."

"I guess it makes sense to me," Dana said. "Paris has seen and heard everything in her house. Why wouldn't it be around there?"

Thank you, Dana. "My visions don't lie, Mayo."

"Are you sure you didn't see the creek at all?" Mayo asked.

I held the banana and let my eyes glaze over. Like I was recalling every nuance of my nocturnal experiences. "Nope, just my house lights. Twinkling through the trees." Perfect screaming distance for help. "But don't worry, Mayo. It gets better." I knew I had to give her more or the whole ruse would be up. "Are you ready for this?" I closed my eyes and grimaced like recalling the vision pained me to the core.

I took a peek and watched Dana and Mayo lean in.

"Another doll," I said.

"You saw another doll?" Mayo said.

"Uh-huh. Beth has been sending me the same image over and over again. When we find it, that's where we spend the night."

"You mean . . ." Mayo gripped my shoulder. "We'll be able to see it, too?!"

"I think so." I hoped so.

"Really?" Dana looked like she was about to cry.

But Mayo lit up like someone had just given her a puppy. "I can't wait!"

Before the bell rang for class, we headed to the ladies' room. While Mayo and Dana pushed through the door, I stopped by the fountain to get a drink.

As the cool water touched my lips, I thought about my plan, relieved that Mayo was on board. But I was still worried. None of this would work if I didn't get Tom's help.

Someone tapped my shoulder.

I turned.

"Hi," Tom said.

I'd never been so glad to see someone. I wiped my mouth and ignored my quaking stomach. "Hi."

Tom stood a little farther back as though he was in line. "P-P-Paris, we *really* need to talk." His face filled with concern.

"*I know.*" My heart raced as I held his gaze. *He does care about me.* "We'll talk later, okay?"

The door to the girls' room suddenly swung open, and I quickly bent down for a drink. My friends stepped out, and Mayo didn't waste a second to go into attack-dog mode on Tom. "You weren't thinking about speaking to Paris, were you?"

I gulped the freezing water down hard.

"'Cuz you've still got an arm left to break, you know—"

• • •

In the car on the way home from practice, all I could think was, *Gas it, Athens!* I had only fifteen minutes to get to the fishing shack to meet Tom, and I wanted to get there and back before dark. We pulled into our driveway. I beat my siblings to the door, dumped my backpack, and zipped toward the garage for my bike.

"Baby!" Daddy called from the living room.

I turned around and made for the foyer. I didn't have time for this.

"Where you going?" Daddy was sitting on the sofa. A muted cooking show played on the set.

Uh . . . "Mrs. Laney's. I want to get some candy." I started to head out again.

"Baby, wait."

"But—"

"Baby . . ." Daddy sounded irritated.

I came back to the foyer just as Verona and Athens stepped through the front door.

"Everyone, come over here." My father got up and moved to the armchair. "Your daddy want to talk."

How many times did I have to talk to my parents in one week?

Verona tossed her sneaker to the floor. "What'd you do this time, Paris?"

"Wa-wa, son. Come," Daddy said. "You all sit."

My siblings trudged—I dashed—to the couch.

"I think . . ." Daddy said, putting a finger to his chin. "You know what I think?"

I didn't know, but he should think faster. I glanced at my watch. I only had twelve minutes left.

"We need to be more like family."

My brother and sister groaned.

"Your mom can't tell me what you doing except girls' basketball. I think we all go to next game. Like family supposed to."

Athens rested his elbows on his knees and covered his face.

"All of us?" Verona repeated.

"Your brother, Mom, everybody."

Come on, come on.

Daddy leaned forward. "When you play?"

Nobody answered. Verona looked around like she had no idea.

"Tomorrow night," I volunteered.

Verona jabbed me.

"Hey!"

"Wa-wa, stop! See?" Daddy said. "This exactly our problem. We let you go too long like this. No more!

"We show everyone we Pans," he continued. "No fighting, just smiles."

My siblings scowled.

I glanced at my watch again.

"You hear me, Baby?"

I looked at my father. "Yeah, sure. I can't wait!"

When we were finally released from the circle of unity, I told Daddy I'd be back in thirty minutes, maybe sooner, and blazed out of the house. I careened down the hill on my bike, pedaling like crazy. I was racing the setting sun and petrified that I'd missed Tom.

When I got to the shack, it was five fifteen.

I stood my bike near the building and noticed the door was cracked open. *Thank goodness.* I opened the door wider. "Tom, I'm here. Sorry I'm late!" I poked my head in and let my eyes adjust to the dark. I saw the outlines of the rails and the water glistening below.

My breath left me.

The shack was empty.

I was too late.

I shut the door. I pictured Tom going to the trouble of getting himself and his broken arm here on his bike, only to have nobody show up.

I gripped the handles and pushed my bike over the planks. I bet Tom was upset. Even mad. How lame must he think I am? But maybe he would let it go if I just explained. *Yes, Paris, calm down.* He probably would. I mean, he did seem so concerned about me at the water fountain today. And he said he wanted to talk like he really meant it. And friends wouldn't just write each other off if they were a little late, right?

I felt better . . .

Until something occurred to me.

I pictured Tom's face again.

Him saying he *really* wanted to talk.

I stopped and glanced back at the shack.

Maybe he never showed up in the first place.

Maybe he wanted to have THE TALK—the "Paris, we need to talk" talk!—that went along with hounding a boy that had already rejected you once.

It all made perfect sense. I make him a stupid card, then I *call* him, then he tells me he just wants to be my friend, and then I write him another note?! I would want to talk to me, too.

I stood there as the possibility soaked in. I looked across the water. The sun was dipping into the lake, taking my plans for the Dare right along with it.

Now it was just me again.

All alone.

I straddled my bike and tried to forget I was riding through the woods. But I couldn't. I got this bad feeling every branch I passed was ready to snatch me as soon as day wasn't looking. My thighs burned as I rode faster.

I can't do this on my own, I told myself.

When I got to Mrs. Laney's, I saw the *Open* sign and a glimpse of Robin sweeping inside. I came to a stop and caught my breath.

I even considered going in.

But I didn't.

I took one final look around me and biked up the hill as fast as I could.

chapter 20

Today was the day—D-day. I spent my remaining hours freaking out about the Dare, wondering how I was going to save myself. As far as I was concerned, the plan, which I had been so gung ho about, was now the worst plan ever. Without Tom as backup, I had just signed myself up for an entire night with Mayo and Dana, scouring the woods for creepy dolls.

Just before we had to leave for the game, I packed everything I might need for the Dare into a giant duffel: Daddy's DeWalt flashlight, the staple gun, bottled water, dried food, first-aid kit, a Bible. I zipped up the bag and rolled it into my closet.

When I got to the living room, my father was standing in front of the TV wearing a yellow construction helmet with two lights that resembled eyes, electrical wire for antennae, and a yellow shirt and black pants. He must have consulted live bumblebees for his outfit. "I'm ready for the game!" he announced.

At least he left off the stinger.

"This is so wrong," Athens said. He stormed off. Verona cried out at the sight and ran to her room.

Daddy looked down at his feet. "Shoes, right?"

I studied his white sneakers.

"I want to be comfortable."

"Daddy, you look great," I said.

It didn't matter, I told myself. No one would figure out he was my father. I headed for my room.

Wait a second. EVERYONE WOULD FIGURE OUT HE'S MY FATHER.

I shook my head as I walked by my sister's room. I heard Verona wailing, but this time, I thought it was justified.

● ● ●

When Verona and I got to the high school and entered the locker room, our friends swarmed around us. I mean, Verona's friends swarmed around her. Mayo and Dana only looked up.

My sister addressed the group. "Everyone, if you see a Chinese man dressed as a bumblebee, I hired him to promote school spirit. Right, Paris?"

"Uh-huh." Good thinking, Verona. Maybe she did possess more than one brain cell.

While we changed into our uniforms, I couldn't help but think about Tom again, wondering if he might be at the "big game." I could use a little support.

I sighed as I bent down to tie my sneakers. Tom or not, how was I going to get through the game and do the Dare?

I stood up. Then something clicked as I stared at a locker bank.

I thought about Tom and his broken arm.

And all at once, the clouds parted in my head, and the sun shined through.

That was it!

What if I *didn't* get through the game? What if I broke something? It wouldn't have to be that serious, even. Just bad enough to earn me a trip to the ER. Then I couldn't possibly take the Dare, and there was no way Mayo would reschedule and miss a chance to do it on Beth's birthday. Plus, I'd tell her, "You-know-who would want it that way." Mayo and Dana would go on without me. Yes!

While we waited to be called onto the court, I stood next to my friends and mentally rehearsed how the game could go.

I'd let a Washington Giant slam into me. I'd tumble to the gym floor—in slow motion.

My ankle would twist and I'd scream in pain.

"Paris," Mayo whispered beside me. "You ready for tonight?"

Paramedics would rush toward me. I'd say, "I think it's broken!"

I glanced at Mayo and saw the mischief in her eyes.

I'd let them walk me off the court. Then I'd wave good-bye to the team just before the ambulance doors closed.

"Ready as ever," I said.

Mr. Wolcott announced us to the fans outside. "Welcome the Sugar Lake Bumblebees!"

We jogged onto the court and warmed up at the hoop as the crowd cheered. With Daddy's getup, my parents weren't hard to find. They were a few rows up in the stands and smiling. Athens looked like he was attending someone's funeral. *His*.

"And now for our challengers," Mr. Wolcott boomed. "The Washington Giants!"

Boos rose from the crowd. I turned to look. A team of girls uniformed in shamrock green ran out onto the court. My jaw dropped.

They were the shortest girls I'd ever seen.

"Fifth graders," Dana said from behind me. "All of them."

I moved forward in line for the basket. "That can't be!"

"Why not?" Mayo said in front of me. "If we have to play a whole team of eighth graders, it's justice."

How am I going to get crushed by a munchkin?!

The buzzer sounded, and I clenched my teeth. This was going to be harder than I thought. During first quarter, I got into every opponent's face and begged them to fall into me. But the Giants refused to do it. They just handed over the ball. By the time the buzzer went off, Coach Dobson was so impressed with my skills, she asked everyone to follow my lead.

I didn't fare any better during second quarter. I decided crashing randomly into fifth graders might do the trick. I fouled four times. Dobson changed her coaching strategy accordingly. She told me one more and I was off the team. I caught a glimpse of Daddy in the stands. He didn't seem pleased.

When Verona and the Bees came on at halftime, the

whole crowd gyrated to *Bzzzz-sting!* for a good five minutes. My sister went all out. Megaphones, wings—they even formed a pyramid. Daddy smiled from the stands.

By fourth quarter, I was out of ideas. I threw myself into the direct line of fire every time the Giants passed the basketball. I suffered from an aching back, sore stomach, and bruised butt. But nothing warranted any medical attention, and the crowd loved me. I glanced at the clock. Seven seconds left. I looked at my fans in the stand—this was my last try. And then I spotted Tom, sitting with Jay.

He's here.

We locked gazes.

He looked away.

My heart crumbled into a thousand little pieces.

Then everything went black.

"Paris!" "Paris!" "Are you okay?"

I opened my eyes. I was lying on the court, head spinning. Coach Dobson and six of my teammates were hovering over me. "Stand up, girl!" the coach said. "Stand up!"

But . . . but . . . where are the medics?

"Paris," Dana said, "you made that one over there mad. She threw the ball at you."

I sat up, rubbing my head. A pint-sized Giant glared at me.

"Foul!" the referee shouted. "One free throw."

The crowd roared.

A hush fell over the gym as I stood at the line. I bounced the ball and summoned the last ounce of energy in my weary body. I didn't care if I made it in. I slung the basketball in the general direction of the hoop. It flew through the air, bounced off the rim, hit the backboard, and sailed through the net.

The crowd brought the house down.

We won 86–6. Sugar Lake set a new record. My teammates lifted me off the ground.

But the only thing I could think was, *Please, drop me now!*

And preferably on my ankle.

It didn't happen.

● ● ●

Before I knew it, Mayo, Dana, and I were in my room, under a mountain of covers, just minutes from doing the Dare.

"You girls sleep good," Daddy said in my doorway. "It almost wear me out watching you play." He pretended to shoot a layup, then he turned off the light and closed the door.

"Time to go!" Mayo whispered, throwing off the blankets. We were all wearing our coats.

"Hang on, Mayo." I tried to stall. "Don't we need to wait until everyone's asleep?"

Mayo stopped for a second as if to think about it. "How long?"

I listened to Verona yammer to someone about the game on the phone. "About two and a half hours."

"No way." She got up.

"Okay, maybe thirty minutes. At least until my parents are asleep."

"Mayo, it can't hurt," Dana said.

"Fine." Mayo collected one of the unzipped sleeping bags at our feet. "We'll go in thirty. Let's start putting these back together."

Tick. Tick. Tick. Tick. My clock was digital, but I could hear that in my head as I rolled up a sleeping bag. *Go to the kitchen for something to drink, slip on the tile, and feign injury.* No . . . it's too obvious now. I worked the zipper around the bag. Actually, anything at this moment would be too obvious. I kneeled on the roll while I tugged the straps around the bundle. *Except for maybe sudden death.*

Mayo nudged me. "Do you hear that, Paris?"

"What?" I held still and heard a giggle I knew all too well. "I don't hear anything." I pushed the bag into its carrier.

"Paris, it's clear as day!"

Dana glanced at the window. "I hear it, too."

"We have to heed the signs," Mayo whispered. "Get up!" She attached her sleeping bag to her backpack, slid the window up, and jumped out. "Come on."

I couldn't believe this was happening. I went to my closet. *Didn't I plan?* I opened the door. *Didn't I try?* I rolled out my duffel. *Didn't I deserve a better ending?*

Mayo poked her head back in. "What's that for?"

"Provisions." And I thought the extra load would slow us down.

"I'm not going to help you carry that. Leave it; we're going to miss her." She moved away from the window.

I looked at Dana, who had just finished putting her bag together. I stared at our backpacks. "We have to move some of this stuff. Hurry."

Dana whispered, "Do something, Paris."

I unzipped the duffel and pulled out everything. "What do you think I'm doing?"

"I mean, stop her."

"What?" I was confused. "I thought you wanted—"

Her voice was tiny. "I know, but this is too much!"

I tried to remain calm as I emptied my backpack. "We'll get through this, Dana, just like you said. All of us. Together. Then we'll carry on like normal, right?"

"Yeah." She started emptying her bag. "But how?"

"Put your hands together."

She did as she was told.

"Now pray."

"But . . ."

"You have any other ideas?"

She shook her head.

"Now it's about survival." I chucked the dried fruit, the water, and the first-aid kit into my bag. "Pack the power tool. It'll fit in yours."

Dana and I helped each other out of my room. I left the window open in case we were lucky enough to return. Then I whispered as loud as I could, "Mayo, wait up!"

She was already creeping through the trees. Her jacket glowed white against the dark of the woods.

"Come on!" she said.

Dana and I held on to each other as we stepped into the woods.

Laughter pierced the air.

"Paris," Dana whispered, "are you scared?"

We pushed past branches, and Dana's grip on my arm tightened. I knew she was depending on me. I lied. "No."

Then *bang!*

Dana yelped. I cringed. "Okay, maybe a little."

When we got to Mayo, she was peering through the branches. "She's gotta be in the shed." She crept forward. "You heard the door, too, right?"

"Uh-huh." I held out my DeWalt. "Here, take it."

She pushed the flashlight away. "You think you-know-who wants a spotlight on her? You'll scare her away."

That was my point.

Mayo dug in her backpack and held up her key chain. A flashlight the size of a pen dangled from it. "This is all we need." She flicked it on.

As we followed the tiny beam of light through the woods, the air grew silent, and the only thing I could hear was my heart pounding in my ears. We were now close enough to the shed, I could see the warped boards in the moonlight. The rusted hinges on the door. The foggy windows where someone had written *Hi*. My insides knotted up.

Something or someone rustled from inside.

Mayo turned off her flashlight and reached for the handle.

"Wait," I said. "I'm not ready." Dana crowded next to me. Together, we gripped the DeWalt. I closed my eyes. "Go."

I heard the door fling open.

I flipped on my flashlight.

Mayo and Dana gasped.

I couldn't help it—I peeked.

And what followed was the scariest thing I'd ever seen.

There was Athens making out . . . with *Roxy*?

We screamed.

chapter 21

We ran like crazy, none of us having any idea where we were going. Except AWAY.

I heard Athens yell after us, "You didn't see anything!"

I almost tripped over a rock. *Ugh, flashbacks.*

Finally, Mayo stopped and caught her breath. She pointed her flashlight in my direction.

"That was so disgusting!" she said. "It's going to take me weeks to recover."

I put a hand to my chest. "Try years."

"Hey, Paris," Dana said. "I just thought of something. If your brother and Mayo's sister get married—"

"STOP right there!" I said.

"Well, I was just going to say, you two could end up related. Neat."

Mayo and I stared at each other, then it hit me. "Hey, wait a second. If Athens and Roxy were in that shed, doesn't that mean I could have been hearing them this whole time instead of you-know-who?"

"Maybe," Mayo said. "And so?"

"Well, then, perhaps . . ." I smiled. "I'm not a medium."

Mayo looked like she was considering this. "No, that doesn't explain everything."

"It doesn't?" Dana and I said.

"Um, your visions and the doll?" Mayo replied. "I doubt that came from Roxy or Athens."

Dana and I looked at each other. Shoot!

"Anyway, noises or not, we still need to do this. Unless, of course, you two are scared?"

"Not me," Dana said quickly.

I looked around at the woods. I could barely see the house lights in the distance. My stomach tightened. "Scared? Hardly."

"All right, then," Mayo said. "Let's do this. Paris, where do we go?"

I looked around me again and bit my lip. I pointed Daddy's flashlight at the trees. "Uh . . . it actually shouldn't be too far from here. Just keep your eye out for a doll." My voice was mostly calm, but inside, I was on the verge of a major meltdown. All I could do was hope I had been wrong about Tom. *Please let there be a doll.*

I led them haphazardly through the woods, keeping the house lights in view. Dana stuck with me while Mayo wandered off a bit. Our flashlights swept the ground. After about half an hour, we hadn't found anything. I felt sick.

"Paris," Mayo called, "we've combed this whole area!"

I shined my light in her direction.

She was searching the ground about ten yards away. Her back was turned to me. "We need to go farther."

Dana whispered beside me, "What now, Paris?"

"I'm trying to think of something," I whispered back.

"Paris?" Mayo turned around. "Did you hear me?"

"Yeah, I heard you," I called. "But Beth was showing me a view that looked just like this . . ." I shook my flashlight toward the house. Then something caught my eye. What was that?

A white ribbon was tied to a branch just eight feet from me, slightly above eye level. An arrow scratched into the tree trunk pointed deeper into the woods.

"Ohmigoodness," Dana said.

Tom.

Mayo started to hike over.

Waves of relief traveled through my body. He came through for me!

"Paris," Dana said, staring at the trunk, "was that done with a knife?"

"Probably," I replied. "But don't worry. I think I know what's going on."

Mayo came up to us. "Beth is trying to communicate!" I said.

She traced her fingers over the arrow. "Unbelievable." She pulled a compass from her pocket and referred to her map. "And get this, Paris, the arrow's pointing toward Miller's Creek. Now we're getting somewhere. Let's move it." She broke a glow stick, tossed it to the ground, and started off.

I waited until Mayo was out of earshot, then whispered to Dana, "Everything is under control. Just back me up, okay?"

Dana nodded.

We came to another tree with an arrow, and Mayo

dropped a second glow stick. As we followed the arrow's direction, I looked back. My house lights appeared and disappeared between the trees. I started wondering why we had to go so far in. Where we were would have been just fine.

My footsteps crunched the leaves.

Tom was probably making it far enough so it would feel more real.

I kept moving.

Or maybe . . .

I stepped over a log.

Maybe it was Beth.

Nah.

Or maybe it was a real killer. I gulped. *All "cooled off" and ready for prime time.*

No, no. A doll would be coming up any second.

But something nagged at me.

How would I know it's from Tom?

As we trekked deeper into the woods, I got this nagging feeling someone was trying to tell me something—like what it had been like when Beth was here. I heard my feet snap twigs, my raspy breaths. The air smelled like a mixture of dead leaves and earth. I pictured Beth's grave in a dried-up creek bed. *Stop it, Paris.* My heart hammered in my chest.

"What the . . . ?" Mayo stopped suddenly.

Dana bumped into her and gasped.

I pointed my flashlight toward the ground.

At our feet was a doll, lying faceup. Eyes closed.

Instead of rejoicing, I held my breath.

Something about it didn't feel right.

"That's weird," Mayo said.

"What's weird?" Dana looked at me.

Mayo nudged the doll with her foot. "I think this is plastic. It should be porcelain."

Did I put that in the note?

I scanned the trees around us.

"Paris, what have you done?!" Mayo's light shined in my face.

I put up my hands. "Cut it out!"

"You did this, didn't you?!"

"I can't see!"

Dana stood between us. "Stop it, Mayo!"

I heard a twig crack.

"Dana, get out of the way!" Mayo shouted.

I turned toward the sound and blinked to focus. *Tom?*

"Paris didn't have any visions," Mayo said. "And I bet she pushed the Ouija pointer, too!"

I swept my flashlight through the trees.

"That was no evil spirit—it was her!"

I heard Dana protest. Then I saw something.

Among the branches.

I made out a girl's face; her eyes glowed white from the reflection of the light.

I knew who it was right then.

"BETH!!" I screamed, yanking at Mayo and Dana. "It's Beth! Run!"

I headed for the soft green light of a glow stick.

Mayo and Dana raced behind me.

I heard Mayo yell, "She's coming after us!"

I ran faster. "Go! Go!" I didn't care what the girl had to say to me.

I pictured that lost face. I passed another glowing marker and made out the next.

Those eyes. My blood ran cold.

More screaming.

I pumped my legs harder.

My house lights burned brighter through the trees. I jumped over a log, but my foot caught a limb. I lost the flashlight as I hit the ground.

"Paris!" Dana shouted behind me. "Get up, get up!"

I spat leaves from my mouth and squinted in the light of the DeWalt.

Dana stopped and tried to pull me to my feet. My ankle buckled from under me.

Mayo ran past. "LEAVE HER!" she shouted. "Beth's coming!"

Dana and I locked eyes.

"Go," I said.

But Dana wouldn't release me.

"I SAID, GO!" I pushed her off.

"I'll get help." Dana glanced over her shoulder, then ran.

Footsteps pounded the leaves, coming toward me.

I couldn't breathe. My eyes burned from the beam of my flashlight.

The footsteps came faster.

Suddenly, I pictured a girl at my window.

Tap, tap on the glass.

I heard crying, sobbing. I couldn't keep sounds and images from flooding my mind. The doll and its cracked face. The marble eye. Beth hiding in the closet. I tried to get up again. The shed door was opening . . . I couldn't get up. *Tap. Tap.*

I froze.

I could see her for real now.

A silhouette among the trees.

There was nothing I could do but scream.

chapter 22

Something grabbed me. My eyes were shut, and my scream carried through the woods. Then I realized someone was saying my name. Shaking me.

I opened my eyes.

In the moonlight, I made out the paleness of a girl's face. *Robin's* face.

I sucked in a breath. I was so relieved, I started crying.

She said the same words over and over again as she helped me up. "I'm sorry, I'm sorry . . ."

When my tears subsided, we were halfway to my house. I had one arm around Robin's shoulders as I limped with a sprained ankle through the woods. Half of my brain was thinking about the pain of my injury, and the other half was sorting out why Robin was here tonight. How had she known about my plans—plans I had only told Tom about in my notes?

My notes.

We pushed forward through the woods. "Robin," I said quietly, "you've been getting my messages, haven't you?"

I felt Robin stiffen. She didn't say anything. But that answer was enough for me.

"You don't have to be sorry," I said.

"Paris?" I heard Verona calling me. A small beam of light weaved in and out of the trees.

When she spotted us, she marched our way.

"Paris!" She shined Mayo's pen flashlight at my face, then down to my feet. "What did you do?"

"I'm fine," I said. "It's just my ankle."

Verona scowled. "Robin, you can let go of my stupid sister. I got her."

I thanked Robin and let Verona take me. Before I could say good-bye, my sister started moving me toward the house. "Do you know what happened, Paris? *Do you?*" she muttered. "Your friends burst into my room while I was talking on the phone; they scared the crap out of me!"

I didn't say anything. I tried to look back for Robin, but I couldn't see her.

"Dana said you needed help," Verona went on, "but Mayo said you'd be home any second. Tweedledee and Tweedledum couldn't get the story straight, and then I heard screaming . . ."

She lectured me the rest of the way. "Listen up, Paris, in case you missed this news flash, those friends of yours aren't worth a penny. Do you even know where they are right now?" We broke through the trees.

I didn't answer.

Verona let go of me, and I leaned against the house for support. "Well, they're not with you, are they?" She pulled off my pack and chucked it through her open window.

"And why are you hanging out with the Freak anyway? You know better." She sat on the ledge and took off her shoes.

"She's not a freak," I mumbled.

My sister climbed inside, then made me sit on the window ledge with my feet facing her. She worked off my sneakers. "Paris, will you just give up already?"

"Give what up?"

Verona stopped her fussing and looked at me.

"Stop wasting time trying to have real friends. It's obvious how bad you want it. You might as well hold up a sign and advertise *Will Work for Friends*. You've got it backward, Paris. Learn from the master." She peeled off my sock. "Find people who will work to be friends with you, and you're better off. Trust me."

Verona studied my ankle and grimaced. "What are you going to tell Mom?"

I shrugged.

She shook her head. "Paris, you're going to owe me big. BIG. Stand up."

I let my sister do whatever she wanted. She took me across the hall for a washing, grabbed my pajamas from my room, and made me change in the bathroom. "Tell Mom you must have sprained your ankle at the game, and make it good."

Verona helped me to my parents' room, and we relayed our story to Mom. From her bed, she told us to put ice on it. "You don't need doctor, right?" she said through a thick haze of sleep.

"What, Doro-see?" Daddy said, sounding as tired as Mom.

"Nothing, Frank," Mom replied. "Go to sleep."

Verona took me to my room, where Mayo and Dana were lying on the floor under the blankets.

"Paris," Dana said, "are you okay?"

I got into bed.

"I'm fine." I winced as Verona slapped a bag of ice on my foot.

"See, Dana?" Mayo said. "I told you."

Verona made a disgusted sound, hit the lights, and shut the door.

"Paris," Mayo whispered. "Do your parents know what we did?"

I took a deep breath and closed my eyes. But all I could hear was Mayo's voice ringing through the woods—"Leave her!"

"Paris," Mayo pressed, "did Beth look anything like her picture?"

I kept my mouth shut.

● ● ●

The next morning, after Mayo and Dana went home, Mom took me to a doctor, much to her chagrin, and I got a set of crutches and my ankle wrapped in a boot.

On the way home, I sat in the front seat, contemplating my situation. Once again, my friend equation was an exercise in fractions (Go = 1/2). Dana hadn't given me any indication she was going to drop her lifelong pal for me, and Robin . . . well . . . I wasn't even sure she'd want to be friends after last night's fiasco, after putting her through all that. And Tom, *Tom* . . . I clutched my midsection . . . he probably thought I'd been ignoring him this whole time. It's official—I win the prize for being the dumbest person alive.

And to top it off, my own mother was mad at me. Ever since she realized this morning that I required medical attention, she'd been tight-lipped. I glanced at my frowning mother at the wheel. *Doctor bills.*

I couldn't live like this.

"Mom!"

She flinched as she drove. Even I was surprised by my own voice. I toned it down. "I'm sorry, okay?" I thought an apology might make everything better. "Now, would you not be mad?"

Mom glanced at me, then stared straight ahead. "What you sorry for?"

"Uh . . ." I stared at her. What wasn't clear here? I pointed at my boot. "My ankle."

"Just ankle? Is that all?"

I was confused. "Yes."

Mom mumbled in Chinese.

"What?"

She translated. "That's not only thing you should be sorry for."

"It's not?" I looked through the windshield and tried to

figure it out. Was she still mad about that dinner when I accused her of wanting Daddy to die?

I gave that one a try. "Well, then I'm sorry about dinner the other day."

"That's not it, either."

Now I was getting frustrated. "Well, what else should I be sorry about?!"

"See?!" Mom said. "I know you not sorry. You don't even know what you sorry for."

"But I am sorry. Honest!" I was sorry for starting this stupid conversation in the first place.

"Honest?" Mom tightened her grip on the wheel. "Now we honest, too? You know what that means?"

I crossed my arms and stared at the glove compartment. "I do."

"How often you practice violin?"

Uh-oh.

"How often, Honest Girl? Tell me."

"Ummm . . ."

"You think your mother don't know? Is that it?"

"Ummm . . ."

"You think I was born tomorrow?"

"Yesterday," I corrected.

Mom slapped the dashboard hard. "Oh, that's right. You smart, too. Always right. Mother always wrong!"

I stayed quiet.

"You don't say any more until you tell me everything."

"Everything? What are you talking about?"

"You can't remember? I help you when we home."

I slouched in my seat. *Double uh-oh.*

• • •

When we walked in the house, Daddy saw my crutches and told me what a big athlete I was. "Baby!" he said, knuckling my cheek. "You take one for team, huh?"

Then he noticed Mom's face. "What, what I do?"

My parents practiced more Chinese.

I got it this time. I was dead.

"Doro-see . . ." Daddy pleaded. "Be gentle. She already hurt."

Mom ignored him. "Baby, go to my room."

Wonderful. I knew what would happen next. She and I would walk inside, she'd shut the door, and there would be no witnesses.

Once I was "secured," Mom went to her dresser. She pulled out a plastic bag and tossed it onto her bed. "I try to put away violin and I find this."

I stared at the bag. Trapped inside was the doll.

"But . . . that's . . . that's . . ." *Real?*

Mom pointed. "Who you take this from?"

"I—I—I didn't take it."

"Really?" Mom said as she pulled the doll from the bag. "Then who's this?"

She flipped the back of the doll's dress inside out and showed me the tag. Two initials were sewn into the tag. "Who B.C.?"

I swallowed. "It's not mine. It's—"

"Athens say yours."

"Huh?!" Wait a second. So my brother did lie. My hands wrapped into fists. *Why?*

"Whose doll? Tell me."

"It's Beth's."

"Who?"

"She's dead, Mom."

My mother's eyes widened. "Wha?"

"Beth Conlon," I reminded. "The girl who DIED here?"

"Ah, I see." Mom's voice turned eerily calm. "If this Beth's, then she own this, too, right?"

She dug in her dresser drawer and pulled out Daddy's staple gun. She dropped it on the bed. "And this?" Next came the DeWalt flashlight.

"And this?!" Mom fished out her Polaroid camera that I had kept in my nightstand. "All Beth's?"

I didn't even have a chance to talk before she burst into tears.

"I work so hard to raise good children—this what I get? You steal. You lie. Why, Baby?" She yanked tissues out of a box on her nightstand. "I tell Daddy what I think and he say, 'Doro-see, maybe Baby play scavenge hunt.'" She sank onto the bed. "What scavenge hunt? I say. Take thing from us, take thing from little girl. Make no sense. Then I look at you, and I see you hiding something from me." She pointed a wadded tissue at me. "Your eyes—I see! Your mother knows . . ." Her nose was stuffed up, and her voice started to sound funny. "I even come to your room. Give you chance to tell me. But you don't. What I do, Baby? What I do I don't deserve truth from own daughter?"

Now she was making *me* mad. I wasn't going to let her guilt me into submission like this. "What did you do?" I said. "*Nothing,* that's what."

I felt the heat building in my face and I couldn't stop myself. "You never ask me how I am. You never ask me how I feel!"

My eyes blurred up so much I couldn't see.

I buried my head in my arms.

The room got quiet.

I tried to stop the tears, but I just couldn't.

Finally, my mother said, "Baby?"

I heard her step over.

"Mom, don't." I was living up to my nickname for once, and I knew it.

My mother swept back the loose strands of hair from my face.

I looked up.

I'd never seen the lines in Mom's face any deeper than they were now. She put her arms around me. I couldn't remember the last time she'd done that, either. "I'm sorry, Baby," she said. "Sometimes I so busy I forget say things." She sighed into my hair. "But you know I never forget you, right?" She pulled back and smiled. "I can never forget my baby."

"I know, Mom." And for whatever reason, that was all I needed to hear. I rested my head on her shoulder. "You do deserve the truth . . ." That was how I started.

I told her everything.

When I was done, I felt fifty pounds lighter and about as old as a giant tortoise. The expression on Mom's face now was one of disappointment and horror.

I could live with that.

"Baby," Mom started, "no more you-know-what."

"I know." I shook my head. "Believe me, I know."

"Now, after all this," she said, "what you do?"

I gave her a blank look and sighed.

"Your mother give you plenty time to think about it."

"What do you mean?"

"Grounded. One month."

"Thanks," I mumbled.

I needed that. And that was the truth, too.

● ● ●

That evening, I sat in my room and tried to make sense of everything that had been happening the past few weeks. I had most of it figured out. All the noises I'd been hearing—the giggling and the voices? Just Roxy and Athens and their sordid outings in the woods. *Disgusting.* The Valentine's card? Probably not Tom, but Robin. And the doll? I picked up the wretched thing from my desk, now back in its plastic bag. So what if this belonged to a dead girl? Or even a killer? *It's just a doll.* I wouldn't read anything more into it, especially now that I'd proven to everyone I was no brighter than a slug.

For the next hour, I concentrated on a plan that would

restore my dignity to the people that mattered. I drew a chart and everything. Then I took it to Mom; I was going to need wheels.

She looked up from her books and approved the document only after she struck step four—*Have Mom make Paris a well-deserved sundae with whipped cream and fudge sauce.* She wrote in a replacement, which I had to admit was a little better.

Then Mom called for Athens. "He drive you."

Great.

I couldn't wait to see him again.

● ● ●

My brother threw my crutches in the back and got into the driver's seat. "I can't believe I have to spend Sunday night carting you around." He shut the door.

"Hmmph." I couldn't find it in me to give him more than that.

"Not talking, is that it? I don't blame you." He started the car, flipped on the heat, and pulled the car out of the driveway. "Mom caught me up on the whole story . . ."

I kept my mouth shut. I was not speaking to him. *Ever.*

". . . Ghosts? Killers?" He held back a laugh.

My face burned as we drove down the road. I reminded myself of my oath. *Not a word.*

"I mean, I knew you were dumb, but come on."

That did it. "You lied to me."

"What?"

"You're a big, fat liar!" I shouted. Was that loud enough?

"Paris, what are you talking about?"

"You don't remember? You lied about the doll." I leaned against the window. "Do you know what *you* put me through?" I liked how that sounded.

Athens stopped the car.

"Hey!"

My brother stared at me. His voice was low. "That wasn't my fault. It was Mom's idea. She didn't want me to tell you she'd found the doll. She said if something funny was going on with you, she wanted you to come to her on your own. And don't say I didn't give you an opportunity to fess up anyway. Because I did."

"Yeah, but you're my brother," I pointed out. "Your allegiance should be to me, not Mom. That's like sibling law or something."

"Is that so? So where's *your* allegiance, Paris?"

"What are you talking about?"

"What else do you want to lie to me about? Hmm? What else do you have on Roxy?"

Uh-oh.

"Are she and Ty going to run off to Hawaii? . . ." His voice got louder. "No, that's not good enough. Is Roxy already engaged? No, no . . . She's a mother of three, isn't she, Paris? You have no idea what you put *me* through. Last week all I did was fight with Roxy over your false information, and then when I realized you'd made the whole thing up, I had to grovel to get her back!"

"All right, fine." I crossed my arms. "We're even."

"Good." He put the car in drive and we continued down the slope.

"Man, Paris, I'm disappointed in you. Don't I deserve just a little more respect?"

"Respect?" I rolled my eyes. "For you? That went years ago."

"That went years ago?" Athens laughed. "Well, check you out. You're all grown up."

The Johnny's Bait and Tackle sign came into view.

"You're *twelve*," Athens said. "Act your age."

"I am acting my age." I sensed my lip trembling. Now was not the time to get emotional. Not in front of my brother.

Athens parked the car in the lot and cut off the engine.

"Paris, look at me."

I pretended I didn't hear him.

"What's with you?"

I didn't know, but I was about to lose it.

"Paris, you're starting to scare me."

I clenched my teeth. *Don't be weak. This is your brother, not Mom. You are not a baby.*

My brother turned me to face him. "Spill it, Paris."

I looked at him and suddenly, my stomach felt hollow; I pictured an empty chair at dinner—his. Verona driving me to school. The Pan Five a Pan Four. "Do you have to go far away to college?" I blurted.

Athens tilted his head at me. "Is that what this is all about?" He sat back. "Since when do you care where I go?"

"Since I realized it's only going to be me and . . ." I shuddered. "And Verona."

"So this isn't really about me, is it?"

Even though it was, there was no way I'd admit that. "Not exactly."

"Good, you had me worried you were getting mushy." He bopped me on the head.

"Ow!"

"You'll be fine without me."

"How do you know?"

My brother smiled. Like a real smile. "Because you're not as dumb as I say you are. Now get going before I freeze to death."

● ● ●

As I made my way toward Robin's house, I took my brother's vote of confidence with me. *I'm not as dumb as he says I am*—it was one of the best compliments I'd ever received.

I went up Robin's steps and crossed the porch. The front of the house was dark, but light glowed from behind the curtain. I rang the bell and I saw the silhouette of Mrs. Laney coming to the door. More lights turned on. "Who is it?"

"It's Paris," I called.

Mrs. Laney undid the locks and brought me inside.

"Paris . . ." She looked at my crutches. "What happened to you?"

"Just a sprain," I said. "Basketball."

"A sprain? Poor thing . . ." She peered out the door. "Is your dad out there? Did he need something?" She headed for the candy racks.

"No, Mrs. Laney. I came to see Robin."

She turned. "Robin?"

I nodded. "I wanted to tell her something."

Mrs. Laney smoothed her apron. "I'll get her. You stay right here."

I rehearsed my lines in my head until Mrs. Laney returned with her daughter. "Paris wanted to see you, honey." She pushed Robin forward, winked at me, and exited the room.

Robin studied the floor and fidgeted with the sleeve of her blouse.

Step one. Here goes. "I'm sorry, Robin," I said.

She looked up, confusion on her face. "Why?"

I sighed. I thought back to Robin standing behind the register and me just standing there. Then the library. Mayo spelling out *freak* in the glass. "I could have done more . . . about Mayo . . . Instead, I just let it go."

"But Paris," Robin said, "you did a lot."

I wrinkled my face. "I did?"

"You *stopped* her. Twice."

I looked at her, wondering how she could stand being

bullied all the time. Then I realized something about Robin. She was much stronger than me.

"I wanted a chance to help you back," Robin said softly. "I realized the notes weren't meant for me. But . . . I thought if you knew it was me . . . I wouldn't get that chance."

I felt uncomfortable with myself once more, knowing she was right.

"I guess I was hoping that maybe we could . . ."

"Be friends?" I said, thinking of the V-Day card.

Robin bit her lip. "I screwed things up, though, didn't I?"

"Actually," I said. "You did me a favor. Trust me."

"I did?"

I nodded, then leaned one of my crutches against the door and dug inside my coat pocket. I held out a square of paper.

"What's this?" Robin said.

"This note is meant for you."

I handed it to her, then watched as she read the note. A smile spread across her face.

It was a simple line, but it captured everything I wanted to say.

I just want to be your friend, too.

chapter 23

The next day, I crutched into the classroom.

"Whoa," Jay said, eyeing my walking aids. He looked across the aisle at Tom. "The whole class is going cripple."

"Jay!" Mrs. Wembly said.

I ignored Jay and glanced at Tom. My heart puddled inside my chest. I hobbled past their rows and spotted Dana and Mayo. Mayo waved from the back.

I stuck my chin in the air and executed step two. I handed my crutches to Mrs. Wembly and took a seat behind Robin. Someone gasped.

"Class," Mrs. Wembly began, "today we begin a new unit: geometry."

Finally. Grown-up math to take my mind off things.

"Let's begin with the basic properties of the circle."

Never mind.

• • •

At lunch, I continued my plan and passed Mayo and Dana on the steps.

"Where do you think you're going?" Mayo asked.

I ignored her and kept moving.

"Paris!" Mayo said. *"You'll regret this."*

I stopped at the last step and turned. "Oh, really?"

"Yeah."

I narrowed my eyes. *"Bring it."*

Dana's jaw dropped.

"Oh, and Dana?" I said.

She seemed surprised I was addressing her. Maybe even a little afraid. "Yes?"

"When you decide who's in control of what you do, let me know. You're welcome to join Robin and me at the tree."

I swung myself around without giving Mayo another look and headed across the yard.

Step three was under way. When I approached the chain-link fence, I counted the kids sitting on the benches. Seven boys. They were all there. *Great.*

Tom noticed me first but didn't say a word.

"Well, look who's here—" Jay said.

"Can it, Jay," I said. "I want to speak to Tom."

All the boys looked his way. One whistled.

I looked Tom in the eyes and felt my stomach introducing itself to the ground again.

"I'm s-s-sorry," I said. *Now who was stuttering?*

Snickers rippled through the group.

"F-F-For what?" Tom said.

I'd start from the top. "I'm sorry for hanging up—"

Tom's eyes bulged out of his head.

Oohs traveled through the crowd. My voice faded. *Maybe I'm not doing this right.*

Jay raised his brows. "If I'm not mistaken, these two need privacy." He stood up and pointed at a sixth grader. "Looks like Debbie is giving me the eye. Let's move 'em out!" He led the pack away.

"Paris," Tom said, "you don't have to apologize." He dug a heel into the ground.

I put together my next sentence in my head. *Don't give up.* "Then I'm sorry—"

Tom cut me off. "You don't have to be s-s-sorry about anything. I know you don't like me, all right?"

"Yes, I do—I mean . . . *excuse me?*"

What did he just say?

Tom looked up. "What did you say?"

"No, um, you go first." My heart started pounding. Was he implying what I thought he was implying? I had to sit down. I propped my crutches against the bench and sat next to him.

"Look, Paris," Tom began, "I know you must think I'm crazy or something . . ."

Go on . . .

"But what was I supposed to think when you sent me that card and then you called me?"

Ohmigod . . .

"And I d-d-don't even know you that well . . ."

Ohmigod—OHMIGOD.

Tom shook his head.

"I even had the f-f-feeling when we met in the fishing shack." He kicked at a rock.

"What feeling?"

Tom stared at me. "Are you trying to be mean?"

"*What feeling,* Tom?" Just say it. Say it!

"Isn't it obvious?" he said. "I like you, Paris. I think I've liked you s-s-since the day you walked into class."

Yes, yes! I couldn't believe it. *He likes me?* I had to be sure. "You like me?!"

"You didn't know?" Tom said.

"How would I know?" I replied. "You never told me."

"It's not like I d-d-didn't try, Paris. Trying to talk to you is like trying t-t-to contact the president. How long can y-y-your phone be busy? . . ."

He tried calling? My hands turned into fists. Verona.

"And when I went up to y-y-you at the water fountain, you s-s-said we'd talk later, but . . . there weren't any notes in the tree. I can take a hint, Paris."

"Tom, wait," I said. "I have to explain."

I told him everything—well, the abridged version; recess wasn't *that* long—and when I finished, Tom let out a breath. "Jeez. You really know how t-t-to mess things up."

"Thanks a lot," I said. But that wasn't important. He liked me. HE LIKED ME. "I still owe you an apology."

"No, you don't."

"Yes, I do. I shouldn't have treated you . . . like . . . like . . . I don't know . . ."

"Like I'm some s-s-sort of embarrassment?" Tom offered.

"Yeah." I cringed. "I guess I was afraid of what people would think."

Tom didn't look a bit fazed. "It's because I h-h-hang out with Jay, isn't it?"

I glanced at his friend talking up the sixth grader in the school yard. *Sick!* "Not exactly."

"It's because people think I'm b-b-brain-damaged, then, right?"

I swallowed. "Sort of."

Tom burst into laughter.

Hey. "I don't think that's funny."

"Yes, it is."

I was confused. "Why?"

"It t-t-took a lot to finally admit I liked you."

"It did?" I stared at him in disbelief.

"P-P-Paris, no offense, but all my friends think you're sort of a g-g-geek. And you hang out with M-M-Mayo."

Oh, man.

I stared at my ankle; this killed more than the sprain.

"Aw, Paris." Tom nudged me with his elbow. "I d-d-didn't mean to hurt your feelings."

I didn't say anything for a second, then sucked it up. "It's okay."

"Hey," Tom said, looking at me. "You're kinda cute when you're s-s-sensitive."

I contemplated whapping Tom's broken arm with my crutch.

But I held back.

I was above PDA.

After talking to Tom, I felt like a whole new person. And when I went to Robin's tree, I barely even noticed the other kids staring at me as I entered the Freak Zone. It didn't matter what they thought. No one could touch me anymore. Not even Mayo.

Robin looked up from her book as I joined her at the tree.

"Paris!" Dana called.

She was running up to us. "I'm coming."

I looked over at Mayo on the steps. Her surprised face was worthy of a Polaroid.

I wished I had the camera.

● ● ●

Step four was the hardest of all. On my chart, Mom had written, *Show you come from one place, go another.* This was her attempt at saying, "Do something symbolic." (Mayo would have *loved* that.) Mom was right. I needed to bring closure to this Dare business so I could start fresh again.

The question was, *What?*

● ● ●

Over the course of the next couple of days, my friends and I brainstormed ideas. Dana suggested we have a party as a farewell to Beth. Tom thought making a hand-made card for you-know-who might be helpful. He was kidding. And Robin thought it was something I should figure out on my own.

Ultimately, I did come up with an answer.

Or maybe the answer came to me. On a windy night. As I was just slipping into bed.

Eeeeeeeeer.

I sighed. I went to my window and yanked up the blinds, prepared to tell my brother to take it elsewhere.

But when I saw what I saw, I froze.

The shed door was standing wide open. Not a sign of my brother and his girlfriend.

I leaned against the wall.

That thing might as well have had step four written all over it.

I reached for the cord and dropped the blinds.

I'd have to go in.

The Dare wasn't over—*yet.*

• • •

That Saturday, I went to the shed.

With my dog.

And the cordless from the kitchen.

And the flashlight.

And the staple gun.

I crept toward the building, backpack on. Go was on her leash. When I reached my destination, I paused before I opened the door. I told myself, *It's just a shed, just a shed.*

"Go, you ready?"

She looked up at me.

I gripped the handle. *This is it.*

I flung open the door.

Nothing horrendous greeted me. The interior space of the shed was no bigger than my bathroom. I only saw some dusty shelves, a few empty buckets, and an old, wooden workbench.

It was all very anticlimactic.

In fact, I may have been a little disappointed.

What was I afraid of?

I took in a deep breath and sat on the bench. I figured if I could stay here for five minutes, step four would be done, and my life would start anew.

I let my watch tick the seconds off, and for about ten of those seconds, I even pretended I couldn't hear the sound of Go growling. But when I felt something bump into my ankles, I yelped and jumped up.

Go popped out from under the bench. She stared at me, then went back to what she was doing.

I watched dirt fly as Go dug.

I knew then.

Beth really was trying to communicate.

But before I could run out of there screaming, Go dragged out a piece of dirty blue fabric. I stopped to look at it. *Oh.* It was just a rag or something.

I took in a breath and glanced at my watch. One minute left. *I can do this.*

Go headed back to the bench and pulled out the rest of her find.

That's when my knees felt weak and my head swirled. *That's no rag.*

It was a girl's shirt.

Mayo's voice echoed in my mind. *"And here's the juicy part. They only found 159 out of 206 bones . . ."*

Go went back to work.

"Makes you wonder where the rest is, huh?"

The dirt kept flying.

It couldn't be . . .

The sensible me spoke. *Get ahold of yourself, Paris. Go found a shirt. That doesn't mean . . .* Go tugged at something.

Well, you came to the shed for a reason, didn't you? Don't you want to close this chapter once and for all?

I stepped toward the bench. Sweat gathered on my forehead. I got on my knees and stuck my hand under the bench.

I touched whatever Go was pulling at.

It was cold. *Leathery?* I wanted to jerk my hand back. *No, no, you have to finish.*

My fingers traveled over the surface as Go tugged.

With both hands, I gripped the object and yanked hard. I almost fell flat on my back. The thing was already loose. It was just a lid to something. While Go tried to shred it to pieces, I reached in again. I felt the sides of a box that matched the lid, then I worked the whole thing out.

When the box was finally resting on my lap, I felt like I'd

just found the missing piece to a ten-thousand-piece puzzle. This was what I had come here for, wasn't it? A box filled with stuff—a Rubik's Cube, a Magic 8 Ball, a girl's shoe made of clear, rubbery plastic . . . Now *this* I could handle. The last item was a plastic bag. I dumped out its contents: a yellowed piece of paper . . . and a photo.

I swallowed hard.

Beth was frowning at me, wearing a boxy, cobalt blue shirt that looked like the same one Go had found—the one Go was tearing up now. She was standing in front of a house I didn't recognize, and bare trees loomed all around her. I turned the photo over and read the loopy handwriting on the back. *September 30th, 1983. Beth Conlon, age 12.*

I set the photo down and picked up the paper, a page ripped from a notebook.

Dear You,

My history teacher, Mr. Maynard, thought it would be fun if we buried stuff so other people might find it and learn how cool it was to live in the 1980s. He thinks it's the best assignment since our Civil War reenactment. I don't understand what is so great about this since (1) Mr. Maynard will never know if I've really done it, (2) I'll never know if anyone ever finds it, and (3) no one but you will have a clue I broke Mr. Maynard's rule and buried it INDOORS. HA!

Here are the things I have included. All of which I didn't mind getting rid of.

I read the list, which included a description of her younger brother's Rubik's Cube, a broken Magic 8 Ball, a jelly shoe that always cut off her circulation, and the shirt that was a horrible color on her. Then I got to an item that actually meant something to me.

5. Genuine hand-crafted Millie Miner doll—my grandmother sends me one of these every birthday. Have you seen anything freakier? I hope in whatever year you're living in, they still aren't making these things and advertising them as gifts. This version of Millie is hideous!!! Especially since I "accidentally" dropped her and broke her face. Oops!
I am so happy this Millie is joining the five million others I've buried all over Foster's Woods.
R.I.P., Millie Miner, number 5,256,539!
Yours, Beth

I pictured the doll I still had. She was safe in the garage. Locked inside a metal toolbox. Wedged under a gigantic table saw.

Then I thought of the "marble" outside my window. There was another one? My stomach turned as I glanced out at the woods. They were *everywhere*.

I returned Beth's letter to the chest and was struck with inspiration. *Do something symbolic.*

Step four wasn't finished.

● ● ●

We picked a spot in the woods where the ground was clear and the surface was flat. Tom, Robin, and Dana helped me dig a hole large enough for everything to fit.

"Staple gun and flashlight," I said.

Tom slapped the items into my hands.

I pretended I couldn't hear Daddy's big sigh in my head as I dropped them in.

"Earmuffs."

Dana gave them to me. In they went.

"Millie number one."

Robin handed me the doll.

"Millie number two."

The one outside my window.

I reached into my pocket and pulled out a plastic bag with a Polaroid zipped inside—a picture of Tom, Dana, Robin, and me standing outside my house. I didn't need it in my album to know I had friends. The proof was already with me.

There was one last thing. I needed to leave something that explained what the items were all about, like Beth had. I dropped in my notebook filled with the details. It begins like this:

Where should I start? The first time I felt my life hanging in the balance? Or the moment I believed the deceased had a way of talking to me ...

After we patted the last of the dirt in place, I planted a cross into the ground made out of orange Creamsicle sticks.

There.

We admired our work.

Step four was done.

Before we got up to leave, I glanced at the branches above our heads. The sun filtered through.

I couldn't help but think I really had brought something to a close. In more ways than one.

Tom helped to me my feet.